Also by Bob Stockton

Sea Stories

Tales told by an old school, politically incorrect Navy Chief

Bob Stockton

First published by Dog Ear Publishing
4011 Vincennes Road
Indianapolis, IN 46268
www.dogearpublishing.net

ISBN: 978-1-4575-6318-8

This book is a work of fiction. Places, events, and situations in this
book are purely fictional and any resemblance to actual persons,
living or dead, is coincidental.

This book is printed on acid free paper.
Printed in the United States of America

Bob Stockton

Contents

Foreword

Life in the Navy is certainly not easy—nor is it particularly difficult. It is however, an enticing and extremely rewarding path for those souls willing to take on the challenges it offers with the promise of great rewards. Where else can one leave the doldrums of high school one day and mere months later be sailing across many oceans to foreign lands only known before in books and Hollywood movies? Where else can that same boy say farewell to his high school friends and return a man, wise beyond his years?

The Navy offers that experience. The Navy has always been an opportunity for youth wanting to expand their boundaries well beyond their country's shores to lands untamed and full of danger. The allure of "running away and joining the Navy" has been around for hundreds of years and it will always be answered by those adventurous souls that want more from life than most.

Having spent over twenty-four years in the Navy myself, with nearly thirteen of those years aboard ships, I can attest to the hardships, the stress, and the challenges presented by a life at sea. That Chief Bob Stockton willingly faced these challenges comes as no surprise to me.

I first met Bob when visiting the Navy Exchange in Mayport, Florida many years ago. I am a book fiend, and whenever I see an interesting read I just must stop and check it out. That day was no different. Bob was kicked back in a chair with a Cheshire cat grin on his face sitting behind a table he had set up and was signing copies of his first novel, *Listening to Ghosts*. I stopped and chatted with Bob while he signed a copy of his book for me and we became friends. Now, nearly eight years later I've read all his books and can tell you without any reservation that his writing style and storytelling ability will lead you on many, many adventures - leaving you wanting more!

Bob's ability to take the reader along with his stories is unquestionable. You will feel the energy of life at sea while he recounts his years serving in the Navy in *Listening to Ghosts*, while sailing on fighting vessels nearly two centuries earlier in

Fighting Bob, while living the life of a cavalry officer in the mid-1800s in *Counting Coup*, and finally, while recounting shipboard life during the Vietnam war era in the Zack Martin series- *Stories from the US Navy I and II*, and *The Third Tour*. Bob can captivate his audience and leave them begging for more with each story.

I've known Bob Stockton for quite some time now and can say without pause he is exactly as he presents himself. Bob served in the US Navy when political correctness was the furthest thing from one's mind, when chief petty officers were salty with experience from World War II, Korea and Vietnam. I have no doubt that his new book, *Sea Stories: Tales Told by an Old School, Politically Incorrect Navy Chief* will push the envelope even more, dragging us along on a journey that will keep us all entertained.

Prepare yourself for an adventure that will leave you ready to turn the page for that next chapter!

Shawn R Michaud
Senior Chief Petty Officer, US Navy (Ret)
Line Pilot, Penobscot Island Air

A Note from the Author

*"**When a sailor** goes ashore after a period at sea he wants to accomplish three things: get drunk, get laid and get in a fight. If he manages to do two of the three it's considered a good liberty."*

Those words, spoken by the fictional "Tyke," my diminutive, hell-raising first-class petty officer in "Patsy and the Tyke" describe a very real event that I have set to fiction in this, my second book of short stories, *"Sea Stories: Tales Told by an Old School, Politically Incorrect Navy Chief."*

In fact, the 16 stories found in this book are fictionalized accounts of actual events told by sailors swapping yarns to pass the time during long, boring mid-watches at sea a half-century or more in the past. Some are humorous, some vulgar, some violent, some tragic, some invite the reader to suspend disbelief. All are true – with a bit of "sea story" embellishment.

The embellishment is what makes the sea story come to life. What was just a rather mundane account of an actual event takes flight via the imagination of the storyteller, often told to upstage the sea story previously told by another sailor in the group. This "upstaging," or "one-upmanship" of the previous story is the true essence of mid-watch yarn swapping: a contest of stories to see who can tell the most outrageous tale. One can always tell whenever a sea story is begun: The story almost always begins with: "This ain't no s**t!"

Welcome to a few of my sea stories. Who will be next?

Bob Stockton
March 2018

Cover design by Zachary Stockton

Part One
Short Stories

Moon Rocks

Snake's been gone for more than five years, went to his reward at 80 in the VA hospital up in 'Yooper" country, the upper peninsula of Michigan. Why he chose to go back there with his Filipina wife remains a mystery to me, and probably was to Snake as well. He did have family up there, so I guess that's what finally tipped the scale for him after retiring from thirty years of active Navy service. Senior Chief Operations Specialist (retired) Richard "Snake" Ross, sea-going sailor, advisor to the Navy of South Vietnam, practical joker, hell raiser, shipmate. Above all a shipmate, never to be forgotten.

As for Jess, well he's down in Temple, Texas with his bride. Jess doesn't travel to the reunions much anymore but he's still sharp as a tack, crusty as ever and willing to volunteer to make his town a better place to live in as well as being an advocate for military veterans. Senior Chief Operations Specialist (retired) Justice "Jess" Bigbie, the pride of Dothan, Alabama, sea-going sailor, boxing team manager, advisor to the Navy of South Vietnam, professional lover, friend, shipmate. Above all a shipmate!

As they say down in Texas, "the two of 'em together were a pair to draw to."

*   *   *

Winter, 1972
'*Now, Senior Chief Bigbie* report to the quarterdeck for a visitor.'

Bigbie looked up from the correction he was entering in one of the navigation publications and addressed the OI Division Clerk.

"Let me see who that is, Cisco. Finish this correction for me."

Cisco Lopez, who was thumbing through a skin magazine nodded without taking his eyes from the magazine.

"CISCO!"

Startled, Lopez looked up.

"Yes, Chief?"

"Now that I have your attention put down the damn skin magazine and finish this correction to Notice to Mariners on my desk. I'm heading down to the quarterdeck to see who wants me."

"Sure will, Chief."

"Do it now, Cisco and while you're at it take that damn skin mag down to the berthing compartment before one of the officers sees it."

"Will do, Chief."

Bigbie, the OI Division Chief, left CIC and headed for the quarterdeck of his guided-missile destroyer leader *England* to see who his "visitor" might be. As his old friend and former shipmate Chief "Snake" Ross was running the Shore Patrol Detachment over on North Island, Bigbie thought that it probably was he.

Good guess. There on the quarterdeck waiting for Bigbie was Snake, decked out in his service dress blue uniform, his five rows of ribbons and gold brass jacket buttons affording a colorful, eye-catching contrast to his dark navy blue double-breasted jacket and trousers.

Jess Bigbie gave his longtime shipmate the once-over.

"Damn, Snake, I can hardly take my eyes off you. You going to a funeral or something?"

Snake gave a mischievous grin. Bigbie had seen that grin many times in the past.

"Jess, there's a film crew holed up at the Mission Bay Hilton shooting footage for a new Robert Redford flick. Dust off your blue war suit and let's hop on over there to see if there are any young starlets with the crew that would like to show their appreciation to a couple of ex-navy brown-water warfare advisors from Vietnam."

Bigbie sighed. It was going to be one of *those* liberty episodes.

"Head on down to the Chiefs Mess and wait while I hit the splash locker and put on my blues. Half-hour tops, then I'll be ready to roll."

Snake headed to the Chiefs Mess on the second deck below the main deck and took a seat in the lounge.

Before leaving the quarterdeck, Jess picked up the ship service telephone, selected CIC, and turned the crank.

"Cisco, this is Chief. Did you finish the NOTAM correction? Okay. Skin mag out of there and in the compartment? Good.

"Mister Nootens up there, by any chance? Okay, put him on."

Lieutenant Dan Nootens, the CIC and Weapons Officer, took the phone from Cisco Lopez.

"Lieutenant Nootens here, Chief. What's Up?"

"Sir, I'm heading over on the beach for a while, I'll be back before morning quarters."

Nootens thought for a moment.

"Why not? I'm Command Duty Officer tonight and I can cover the Ops eight-o'clock reports. Anything hanging that I need to know about?"

"No, sir, everything is squared away."

Nootens gave an almost imperceptible nod while he answered.

"Alright, Chief. See you at quarters tomorrow."

* * *

"What? Valet parking? Why are you parking in valet?"

Snake shrugged.

"No particular reason, just easier."

The two Navy Chiefs got out of the car. Snake handed the keys to the kid working the valet kiosk and took the receipt for the vehicle. The two friends entered the hotel, walked directly to the hotel lounge and seated themselves on two empty seats at the bar.

"Gentlemen! Welcome to the Mission Bay Hilton. How may I serve you?"

The name engraved on the barman's name tag which was pinned to his vest suggested that they were being served by Eli. Snake responded:

"Eli, let's have a couple of cold Heinekens if you don't mind. And will you start a tab? We're planning to stay for more than one."

Eli nodded. "Done. Two Heinekens for the U.S. Navy."

The barman moved along the bar to the beer cooler located at the far end, opened the thick glass door and removed two cold bottles of the requested brew along with two equally cold mugs. He deftly opened both bottles and returned to Jess and Snake's location.

"Here you go, men. Enjoy.

"By the way, you guys wouldn't by any chance be from the *Ticonderoga* that docked over at North Island yesterday with the Apollo 17 capsule, would you?"

Jess glanced at Snake, who gently tugged at Jess's jacket sleeve which was at his friend's side and out of the barman's view. He knew that Snake was planning something.

"Eli, my friend," Snake replied, "we are not permitted to speak of where we have been or what we have been doing to anyone not authorized to know."

Eli smiled and nodded his head.

"Say no more, my friends. Your reply has already told me that you are with the recovery team."

"Well," Snake responded, "think what you will but don't expect either of us to confirm what you are thinking."

Eli smiled and winked. His suspicion was confirmed in his own mind. As he was about to reply a young woman entered the bar. She was dressed in rather tight, form-fitting jeans and a T-shirt which bore the Warner Brothers logo on the front. She had an identification card which was laminated in clear plastic and suspended from her neck with a cloth cord. The young woman gave the barman her order, turned to look at the two Navy chiefs seated a half-dozen seats from her and smiled.

Eli returned with her drink order and began to engage the young woman in a whispered exchange, glancing at Jess and Snake.

Motioning to the barman, Snake leaned toward Jess and spoke in a low tone. "Shipmate, let the games begin.

"Eli, ask the young lady if she would care to join us for a drink."

Snake turned and spoke to Jess.

"When she turns to look at us again give her one of your patented smiles."

"Why me? Is it because I'm so much better-looking than your sorry ass?"

Snake laughed.

"No, shipmate, it's because she's sitting on your side.

"Better-looking. That'll be the fucking day."

Eli had delivered the message. The young woman left her seat and walked along the bar to join Snake and Jess.

"Hi, thank you for your offer. I'm Norma."

Jess returned her smile with one of his own and moved one seat to his right, offering Norma his now-vacant seat.

"Hi, Norma I'm Jess and this is my shipmate Snake. Have a seat in my place."

Norma smiled again and sat between the two friends.

Snake turned and grinned at the young woman offering his hand. Norma took his hand a gave him a sturdy handshake.

"Snake. Surely that's not your real name. Why does your friend here say that your name is "Snake?"

Snake shook his head and continued grinning.

"Most of us that work together have nicknames, kind of builds teamwork and familiarity with our team of…

"Better not say any more."

Norma smiled knowingly.

"Oh sure, that's fine. Well, Jess and *Snake*, I'm Norma Seabrook. I'm with the film crew that's here shooting some footage for the new Robert Redford movie that is coming out next fall."

"Says you're an associate producer. That's pretty important, I'd say."

Norma smiled and shook her head.

"Jess, that's just another cleaned-up name for "gofer," believe me. The director or cast needs something, our crew plays fetch.

"It's a cool way to make a living and I'm learning the film-making business from the ground up."

A young man dressed in jeans and a blue polo shirt entered the bar.

"Norma! I've been looking all over for you. I might have known you'd be at the bar chatting up sailors."

"Hello Colin. Say hello to Jess and Snake."

Colin Pemberton, another of the film crew's associate "gofers" smiled and extended his hand.

"Pleased to meet you, men. Which is which?"

Snake raised his hand. "I'm Snake, he's Jess. Glad to meet you, Colin. Is Redford here at the hotel?"

Colin shook his head.

"No, no. We're just here with a crew shooting location shots around La Jolla and a few other places. The cast and director and everyone are in San Francisco where the film will take place."

Norma reached back and gathered Colin's right arm in a gesture designed to capture Colin's focus.

"Colin, guess what? The barman told me that these two handsome sailors oversee the team that will be taking the moon rocks back to Washington. Isn't that exciting?"

Snake's insinuation to Eli the barman regarding his and Jess's faux "mission" was growing with each subsequent re-telling.

"Wow! I'll say! Be right back."

Pemberton hurriedly left the lounge and after a few minutes returned with several members of the film crew.

"This is, uhm Snake and Jess, right? Yeah, I thought so. These navy guys are couriers that will be taking some very specialized moon rocks back to Washington, right guys?"

"Let's have a round of drinks on me."

Snake nodded. "Why not? We're drinking Heinekens."

"Gotta go pump bilges to make room for more beer. Jess, looks like we're gonna be here longer than we intended."

Jess nodded. "Well, it isn't every day that we get to have a drink with Robert Redford's film crew."

The drinks all around arrived shortly after Snake left to "pump bilges."

Colin raised his glass in a toast.

"Here's to our brave servicemen in general and to these two Navy officers who will be leaving soon for a very special space-related courier mission."

After the chorus of "hear-hears" abated, one of the men the film crew ordered another round.

"We don't meet men such as yourselves very often. Let's have another round and get to know one another a bit better."

Jess replied, "I think I can speak for Snake when I say that your offer sounds like a great idea.

"And by the way, we're *chief petty officers*, not officers."

Snake had returned during the exchange. He leaned closer to Jess and whispered, "Follow my lead."

Jess nodded.

After a few more rounds Snake grabbed Colin's shoulder and motioned him to come closer. Taking him by the elbow, he walked him a few paces away from the group who were by this time in full-party mode.

When they were out of the group's hearing range, he spoke in a low voice.

"Listen, you are a really great bunch of guys. If I show you something will you promise me that you won't tell anyone?"

Colin's interest was piqued.

"Why can't I tell anyone?

"You can't tell anyone because if word gets out about what we have done Jess and I could be court-martialed, busted and sent to prison."

"What! What the hell did the two of you do, for God's sake?"

Snake looked around to see if anyone was listening.

"We took one of the smaller porous rocks, the ones that NASA is real interested in."

"Jesus!"

"Yeah, that's right. They'd have our asses if they even *knew* that we were talking about this, let alone having copped one."

"Can I see it?"

"Can I trust you?"

"No problem, mate. Let's have a look."

"I have it in my car. Tell you what, go back to the bar and order us another round while I go to the car and get it."

"No problem, mate. Go on ahead."

After several minutes Snake returned carrying something wrapped in several paper towels. He approached Colin who was by this time feeling very little pain.

"Come over here where we can't be heard."

Colin nodded and walked with Snake over to a booth and the two sat down.

Snake gave a nervous glance around the room to be certain that no one could hear or see what he was doing. He unwrapped the paper towels and held the exposed moon rock close to his lap.

"Cor! I am so fucking glad we met you sailors tonight. This is bloody history!

"Will you let me show this to my friends? I know they'll keep this quiet."

"Colin, we don't have time. I need to put gas in our rental car and we have to get back to the ship."

Colin thought a for a moment then offered a suggestion while pulling out a twenty-dollar bill from his pocket.

"Look, Snake, here's a twenty for gas for your rental car. Let me have the rock for tonight and I'll leave it with the barman and you can pick it up tomorrow."

Snake thought about Colin's proposition.

"Tell you what. We need to be long gone before you start showing this around.

"Best way to do this is through Eli. Let me talk with him about it and I'll see if he'll help us out with this. Go back with your friends and I'll see what I can arrange.

"And don't say anything yet."

Colin nodded, turned and walked back to the bar where the film crew was having a ripping good time while Jess was regaling Norma with tales from the high seas.

Snake walked over to the far end of the bar and motioned for Eli to join him.

"What's up, Chief?"

"Eli, my friend, how have you been doing on tips tonight with my new-found friends from Warner Brothers?"

Eli grinned. "Lights out. Why?"

"Well, it seems that your conversation with the lady has zoned the film boys in to our moon rock theft."

"Uh huh. So?"

"So, I need a favor from you. I told our friend Colin over there that he could show the rock to his friends with him, but I had to leave. and he could leave the rock with you and I'd come back for it tomorrow.

"That alright?"

Eli thought for a moment.

"Hm, I don't know. Let me see the rock."

Snake pulled the paper towels from his jacket pocket and unwrapped the parcel.

Eli looked at the moon rock and smiled.

"Shit! That looks like a piece of one of our urinal cakes. What the hell you got going? Did you pull that nasty thing out of one of the urinals?"

Snake shook his head. "No, man there are some fresh ones stored in the cabinet under the sinks. I took a piece from one of them.

"Look Eli, you made a lot of tips from these film people tonight and Jess and I have taught some kid that his personal desire doesn't trump national security. Look at it that way."

The barman chortled, then agreed.

"Right, but I have never seen this 'moon rock,' okay?"

"Done deal."

Snake dropped the wrapped 'rock' in his pocket, walked over to Colin, retrieved the rock and placed it in Colin's hand.

"You don't show this until we're gone fifteen minutes, right?"

"You got it, mate."

Snake motioned to Jess who was engaged in a heavy conversation with Norma.

"Got to get back to the ship, Jess. Let's go."

Jess said a quick goodbye to Norma, got up and the two men left the lounge, headed for the valet stand.

Later, while Snake was driving Jess back to his ship Jess produced a scrap of paper. The scrap had some numbers written on it.

"Look what I have, shipmate. This is Norma's phone number and address in L.A."

Snake laughed.

"Shipmate after I tell you what went on with that boy from the film crew tonight you might as well shitcan that piece of paper. Ain't gonna do you any good.

*   *   *

Photo courtesy of the Naval History and Heritage Command

A Ticket to Sea Duty

Spring, 1958

It all began for me in early 1958 while I was shacked up with Gloria, a twenty-something hooker from Tio Pepe's bar in Tijuana.

An explanation is in order.

At the tender age of seventeen years and six months I, along with 75 other young Navy recruits had managed to shiver through nine weeks of training during the bitterly cold winter of 1957 at the Great Lakes Naval Training Center (a company wag once opined that during the cruelly cold and dark morning musters on the parade grinder adjacent to our barracks that one could "hock a loogie" and it would be frozen before it hit the ground). During that miserable period in my life a Navy occupation detailer decided that I was destined to become a "Communication Technician, Radio," a specialty that would almost guarantee a four-year enlistment with no sea duty. My protests to the detailer, a second-class petty officer, that I just wanted to go to sea fell on deaf ears.

"Son, you'll be heading to the Communication Training Center at Imperial Beach, California for twenty-four weeks of training when you are finished here. Period."

That was that. At least it's warm in California.

*   *   *

The communication station at Imperial Beach had recently been renamed Naval Security Group (NavSecGru) Imperial Beach. The facility had been in continuous use since before World War II and certain structures, for example my barracks, had been rehabbed to keep them in use for the new trainees which arrived each week. Both the basic and advanced schools were one story concrete buildings, the difference being the barbed wire fence, entry code keypunch and the armed Marine that guarded the entrance to the advanced school where the crypto machines were housed.

The base commanding officer had dictated that there would be no civilian clothes on base for the students in the basic training weeks, and so we "newbies" left the main gate in our dress canvas and walked over to Sid's Locker Club where we could purchase a few shirts and cotton chino slacks for liberty in the area. Sid also had full length lockers available for rent and a locker room where we could change before we left to go looking for love - or something akin to love - in all the wrong places.

Seeing as I was not yet twenty-one I chose to head south five miles to the border town of San Ysidro with a fellow trainee by the name of Terwilligar where we would cross the border into Tijuana. Terwilligar, or 'Tweeg' as his bar girl friend Josephina called him, hung out at a bar by the name of Tio Pepe's where 'Josie' worked as a B-girl hustling drinks from the tourists and sailors that entered the establishment looking for a drink, a meal, a pretty girl, a short-time in the back or all the above. Josie had a roommate named Gloria and after a Cerveza Tecate or two and a few bar drinks for Gloria and Josie it was decided that we'd spend the night with them at the girls' "house," a rundown, cold water shack just off the main drag.

My evenings with Gloria, as delightful and educational as they were for a young and reasonably innocent seven-teen-year old, would hasten the end of a short-lived career as a Communication Technician, Radio. The problem for me was three-fold: in 1958, two of the requirements for moving on to the advanced crypto school were that a student was required to type at a certain speed without error and had also to learn Morse Code while decoding the dots and dashes and typing them on carbon message forms. I could hold my own as far as learning code, but the task of hearing the code signals in the earphones at my desk, decoding the signal and typing the decoded message on a sheet of paper while nursing a Tijuana hangover proved to be my eventual ticket to sea duty.

*   *   *

"Chief Mayo wants to see you in his office. Now!"

Mayo was the basic school director. That one sentence from the class instructor marked the end of my career in naval radio communications. The conversation with the chief was brief and to the point:

"Son, you have failed another weekly performance test."

'Son', I thought, *'How many fathers am I supposed to have in this outfit?'*

"Yes, Chief."

"We have set you back to the beginning class once already. What is your problem?"

I shrugged, thinking it was better to keep my mouth shut rather than tell him how much I disliked the idea of becoming a communication technician, radio.

Mayo leaned back in his swivel chair, appeared to be thinking for a moment or two, then rendered his decision.

"I see no reason to continue your training. I am recommending that you be disenrolled from training and sent to sea."

I nodded, barely able to contain my excitement.

"Go back to your barracks, pack your seabag and report to Boatswain's Mate Second Class Parker in the mess hall. He will assign you mess cooking duty while you wait for your orders to sea."

"Yes, Chief, that all?"

"That's all, son."

I nodded, turned and left his office, free at last from the boring and repetitive training that I hated.

*   *   *

Boatswain's Mate Second Class Donald 'Boats' Parker, the mess decks master-at-arms had been stuck in his boatswain's specialty grade for nine years; there were simply too many of the same specialty above his grade which had "frozen" him from promotion. Because of this he had requested that the Navy shift him to a job that would permit his advancement based on merit rather than fight the logjam in his current specialty. The Navy had approved his request and sent him off to Imperial Beach to train as a communication technician which was "wide open" as far as promotions were concerned. This career shift would also allow Parker the chance to enjoy some shore duty, a luxury that was rarely afforded sea-going jobs such as boatswain's mate.

It was a terrific opportunity for Don Parker and he jumped at the opportunity. There was just one small snag: He, like the rest of us who were banished to the limbo of mess cooking, couldn't, no matter how hard he tried, master the task of converting Morse Code to words and typing them on three-part message paper.

"Well sailor, I figured it was only a matter of time before you joined us."

I nodded. "How are you, Boats? To tell the truth I'm glad to be here. All I ever wanted to do was go to sea, and now I have a shot."

'Boats' Parker smiled. "Well between now and then I need someone to run the dishwashing machine in the scullery.

"You'll be here for about six weeks before your orders arrive. Reveille is at 0400 every day. After each meal is secured you have free time until the next meal, that means usually about an hour, maybe a little bit more between each meal. The galley and mess decks secure at 1800 and cleanup is about an hour. After that you have liberty until the next morning meal. You'll work that shift for three days, then have two days off.

"Got it?"

I indicated that I understood the schedule.

"Alright, then. The barracks is the one-story building just behind the galley. Go see the compartment cleaner and he'll assign you a locker and bunk. His name is Walpole. You know him?"

"Ken Walpole? Sure, I know him. I wondered why I hadn't seen him lately."

"Okay, then. Your master-at-arms will be a second-class gunners mate named Myers. I've got my orders back to sea and will be leaving in two days. Until then I have open gangway liberty and won't be around."

"Where you headed, Boats?"

"Going to a heavy cruiser, the *USS Rochester*, and I'll be damn glad to get there after all of this."

"Good luck, Boats."

"Same to you, sailor. If I run into you somewhere in the Western Pacific, I'll buy you a drink."

*   *   *

Scullery mess cooking. A hot, greasy, nasty job. The worst job in the galley. I had heard stories during boot camp service week about scullery mess cooking and now I was to get a first-hand experience. If that was what it took to get to sea, so be it. I picked up my seabag, left the galley master-at-arms office and headed for the mess cook quarters.

"I figured that it would be only a matter of time before you got here."

The greeting from my friend and fellow washout Ken Walpole had a familiar ring.

We shook hands. "Hey, Ken, how's it going?"

"Not bad. Got a bottom bunk for you if you want it. Where did Parker assign you?"

The look on my face answered his question.

"He put you in the scullery? No shit?"

"Yeah. Said it'd be six weeks before my orders got here."

"Mmmh, that's about right. I've been here about a week and lucked into this job. Sweep and buff the deck every morning and clean the head while everyone's in the galley working breakfast.

"Let me give you a heads up on a third-class stew burner named King. He's got two hashmarks on his sleeve and thinks that eight years in the Navy makes him God. You can't miss him, got tattoos on his earlobes and is tongue-tied. Can't understand a word he says.

"It really pisses him off when we ask him to repeat what he just said. We all do it. Ha! Sends him right up the wall."

* * *

Ken Walpole's assessment of King was spot-on. Eight years had passed since his initial enlistment and King had advanced only one pay grade above the seaman mess cooks working in the galley. He was small in stature, foul-mouthed, covered in tattoos and a terrible cook. His galley chief, Chief Hoskins, was overheard in a conversation with the base supply officer saying that King couldn't even "boil water" without screwing it up. Because of that conversation King was relieved of his duty and sent to work assisting Gunner's Mate Myers in supervising the mess cooks in general and – you guessed it – specifically the mess cooks working in the scullery. Commissaryman Third Class King was to be my immediate supervisor.

"Dod damn it, Sockin, wook at this pot! You need to scwub this pot wif steel wool before you wun it in the dishwashuw. Get some doddam steel wool and scwub the gwease off and wun it again!"

"Didn't quite get that, King, what is it you want?"

It never failed. King's neck would slowly turn a dark reddish hue, while he tried to hold his temper.

"You know doddam well what I said, Sockin. Scwub those doddam pots until they shine, or I will have you wowthwess ass, you boot mothewfuckew."

And so, the time in the scullery passed, day after day, week after mind-numbing week, working fourteen-hour days while listening to King 'want and wave' (translate: rant and rave), lording it over the mess cooks in the scullery.

One evening after a particularly bad day in the scullery, 'scwubbing' pots and pans, I finished up and headed back to the mess cook berthing area. I was greeted by a grinning Ken Walpole.

"Got my damn orders, man. I'm out of here in the morning!"

"Hot damn, Ken, where are you headed? And how about putting a word in for me with Myers? I'd like to take your job and get away from King for the rest of my time here."

Walpole shook his head and showed me his transfer orders. "Might not be enough time to see Myers.

"Going to the *USS O'Brien*, a tin can out of Long Beach. I muster tomorrow at 0700 in front of the admin office to pick up a Navy bus headed for the Long Beach Naval Station.

"If I see him between now and then, I'll ask."

"Destroyer duty. That's the ticket, Ken. I'm hoping for a tin can myself. Maybe I'll get the *O'Brien* as well."

"That would be neat, wouldn't it? You shouldn't be waiting much longer for your orders."

I shrugged. "Hope not. I've had a belly full of King already."

Walpole laughed. "Ain't it the truth? Anyway, if I don't see you tomorrow, maybe we'll hook up sometime in the fleet."

*   *   *

One week, almost to the day after Ken Walpole left for Long Beach, I received word to report to the base personnel office ASAP. I thought that King was going to swoon with apoplexy as I walked out of the scullery in the middle of noon meal clean up. I rewarded him with my A-list 'screw you, asshole,' smile and headed out the galley door for the personnel office a few blocks distant.

"I was told to report here, probably for orders to sea."

The personnel clerk took my name and checked a roster list on his desk. Scanning down the list, he reached my name just beneath mid-point.

"Here it is. You have orders to the *USS Ernest G. Small*, a radar picket destroyer."

I could feel a lightning bolt of excitement surge through my entire being.

"Where is she home-ported?"

"Says here Long Beach, attached to Destroyer Squadron 13."

"Long Beach! Hot damn! I hear that it's a great liberty town! When do I leave?"

"Pack your seabag and muster here tomorrow morning at 0700. There will be a Navy bus waiting to take the transferred group to the Long Beach Naval Station."

I was barely able to contain my excitement. A new and exciting chapter in my life was about to unfold!

Mess cook reveille at 0400 the next morning arrived. King, afforded one last shot at making my life miserable, informed me that transfer or no, I'd be getting "youw ass out of youw bunk now, you mothewfuckew (King's favorite adjective…or is it an adverb? Ah, who cares). You ain't sweeping in hewe today, you been twansfewwed."

I gave him a wide grin, which pissed him off even more, and jumped out of my bunk to wash up. I had packed my seabag the previous evening, which meant that I had only to clip the dozen or so whiskers from my chin, don my dress blues, buff my shoes and head over to the galley at 0600 for breakfast.

The breakfast at the galley that morning was perfect for a soon-to-be seafaring Navy Bluejacket: baked beans, cornbread, hard boiled eggs and coffee. I ate heartily and left the mess decks without so much as a backward glance.

So long Imperial Beach, T-town and Gloria! I was headed for sea duty aboard one of the Navy's storied ship classes, a destroyer!

*　　*　　*

Naval Security Group Imperial Beach

Linton's Fifteen Minutes

Summer, 1958

"Your ship is due to arrive on the 26th. You'll be assigned a bunk in the transient barracks until Destroyer Division 132 returns from their Western Pacific deployment. The barracks master-at-arms will assign you a bunk and a work detail."

The personnel clerk handed me a street map of the base.

"Take the station bus to the transient barracks and check in with the barracks master-at-arms."

I nodded, hoisted my seabag on my shoulder and exited the personnel office for the short ride to the base transient barracks.

The transient barracks master-at-arms was a grizzled old salt, a second-class torpedoman's mate whose name has long since escaped me.

"Looks like you're gonna be here for 12 days, sailor. Check with the compartment cleaner for a bunk assignment, store your gear and report back here to me for a working party."

Working party! An oxymoron if ever I've heard one.

"The compartment cleaner is a kid named Walpole who is waiting for a ship in the same tin can division as yours. He'll assign you a bunk and locker and will issue you a fart sack, blanket and pillow. You'll have to sign for the bedding. If they are lost or stolen it will be taken out of your pay."

'Walpole? Wonder if it's Ken?'

"Tubes, would Walpole's first name be Ken?"

"Maybe. Hell, I don't know. Ask him when you see him.

"Get your bunk assignment, change into your work dungarees and get back here for a working party."

I nodded, turned and left the office, headed for the barracks berthing bay.

Small world. There was Ken Walpole, once again on the business end of a deck buffer.

"Did your recruiter slip a rider in your service record that says you only work as a compartment cleaner when you are waiting for a transfer?"

Walpole grinned. We shook hands.

"So, you finally escaped from King. What ship are you waiting for?"

"Tin can", I said with a grin, "*Ernest G. Small*, Destroyer Division 132."

"Great! The *O'Brien* is in 132 also. We'll probably be tied up alongside each other at the pier."

"You've been here for a while, Ken. Any news other than when the ships arrive?"

"Nothing, other than the division has been in the Western Pacific for the past seven months. The *O'Brien* is the division flagship. Haven't heard much else, although there are a bunch of sailors in the barracks waiting for the same arrival. They're headed for the *Walke* and the *Harry E. Hubbard*, so my guess is that those ships are in the division as well."

Seven-month cruises to the Western Pacific! Exotic, far-away ports with exotic women anxiously waiting for the arrival of a U.S. Navy ship!

I could hardly wait for the next two weeks to pass.

*　*　*

Five days after my eighteenth birthday I was awakened by the sound of the barracks master-at-arms announcement on the public-address speaker.

"All sailors waiting for the arrival of *O'Brien*, *Walke*, *Hubbard*, *Small* muster outside the barracks with your packed seabags at ten-hundred hours."

Our group jumped out of our bunks, turned in our linen to the linen locker, washed up and packed our bags.

The muster outside the barracks front went smoothly and we boarded the bus and departed for the short ride to the pier which had been made ready for the arrival of Destroyer Division 132.

*　*　*

Our replacement group arrived at the designated destroyer pier to find that we were not alone. Waiting pier side for the arrival of the division was a Navy band, several high-ranking Navy officers, families of the returning ships' crews, sailors returning from emergency leave, and several television reporters from the local media outlets along with their camera and sound crews.

About thirty minutes after our arrival at the pier the four destroyers appeared in a single line at the harbor breakwater with *O'Brien*, the division flagship in the lead, followed by *Walke*, *Harry E. Hubbard* and *Small* (I was to learn later that the order of appearance of the four ships were indicative of the ships' captains' seniority which meant that my ship was going to nest outboard of the other three).

The arrival was a sight to behold! The Navy band was playing stirring march music, the four ships had their pennants colorfully flying from the signal halyards, wives and children of the returning men craning their collective necks to catch a glimpse of their loved ones who were returning home after a seven-month absence, all in all it was both an exhilarating and thrilling sight to behold.

At last! I was about to become a seafaring destroyer sailor with a girl in every port! I could already feel the salt spray and smell the salt air as my ship sailed briskly into the wind, bound for exotic ports-of-call!

*   *   *

"My name is Boatswain's Mate Second-Class Linton. I am your division leading petty officer. Your division lead seaman is Granny Miller, who you will muster with down in the compartment when we are done here. Can't miss him, his head looks like it wore out a half-dozen bodies.

"The ship's Bos'un is Chief Cox. Chief Cox oversees the two deck divisions. He is responsible to Lieutenant Youmans who is the ship's first lieutenant. Mister Youmans reports directly to the Captain, Captain Dozier. Remember those names as they are your chain of command.

"Men, you are now standing on the round end of the ship. It is called the fantail. That big gun mount directly behind you is Mount 53. Mount 53 houses two rapid fire five-inch thirty-eight caliber naval guns that we use for either shore bombardment or anti-aircraft defense. Get to know Mount 53, as some of you will man your general quarters battle stations inside her.

"Just forward of Mount 53 you will see an open deck hatch with a ladder leading down to a berthing compartment. That compartment, the 2nd Division berthing compartment will be your home away from home while you are here. This means that you are now a vital part of one of the two ship's deck divisions, the Second Division.

"While we are in port stateside, the Captain has authorized three-section liberty. You will each be assigned to one of those sections. This means that you will be authorized to leave the ship after working hours when you are not in the duty section, been assigned a working party or any other ship's function.

"At 1600 hours on Fridays, one section will have a 72-hour liberty pass and will not be required to return until Monday morning routine at 0530. A second section will have a 48-hour liberty pass. That section will turn to on Saturday morning and conduct ship's work until 1130 at which time they may go ashore for the rest of the weekend, returning for Monday morning routine at 0530. The third section will have the duty weekend and be required to work or stand watches throughout the weekend.

"Now, if you ain't in the duty section I would advise you to haul ass off the ship because if I see you laying around in your bunk, I will put your ass to work. Forewarned is forearmed. Ain't no layabouts in *this* division.

"We will have these liberty hours for the next month. We will then be towed outside the breakwater to a barge where we will offload all the ammo in the ammo magazines and enter the shipyard here for a three-month overhaul. Once in drydock there, we will be putting your young and tender asses over the side on scaffolding and you will be taking the ship down to bare metal with pneumatic paint chippers called needle guns.

"Put your hand down, son. They ain't any time to play twenty questions.

"We are responsible for the main deck and superstructure bulkheads from midships aft to the stern.

'*Shit. Girl in every port, my ass. This guy is gonna work my ass off. I'll be too tired to enjoy the little bit of liberty they give us.*'

After our somewhat less than pleasant "welcome aboard" from Linton, our group turned and headed for the compartment hatch and awkwardly descended the compartment ladder into our new "home away from home." Granny Miller was waiting to assign a canvas bunk and foot locker for us.

You couldn't miss Granny Miller despite the rather disparaging description given us by Linton. Miller was a diminutive 5'4", 100 or so pound black man who looked to be around thirty-five. His undress blue jumper had his three seaman stripes sewn on the upper left sleeve along with three large red "hashmarks" sewn on the lower left sleeve which indicated that Miller had somewhere between twelve and sixteen years of service. I was later to learn that Granny Miller was the longest serving sailor on the ship, having reported aboard for duty in the late summer of 1951and was wounded when the ship struck an underwater mine while conducting shore bombardment during the Korean War. He was also the best helmsman on the ship and an extremely diligent sailor when the ship was at sea. Miller also had a fondness for strong drink when the ship was in port which kept him in hot water with the wardroom and would cost him a stripe or two every so often.

"Bunks is three to a stack, canvas strapped tight to a frame and a tick mattress on top. Put the mattress inside you fart sack and use the pillow and blanket on you bunk. In the morning use the bunk chains to trice up the three bunks so you can get to your foot locker and the compartment cleaner can swab and buff the deck."

'What the hell does he mean, trice up?'

"You new guys that ain't been on a ship before, trice up means that the three bunks on your stack all swing up together in a 90-degree stack. You'll get the hang of it tomorrow at reveille, which for us is 0500. We up and out sweeping and clamping down the deck – that means swabbing – then shining all the brass lifeline turnbuckles and other brightwork before breakfast for the crew. Then we eat, square away our bunks and go topside to muster for morning quarters. After muster we commence ship's work until 1130 when chow go down. After chow, you got a bit of free time until we continue ship's work at 1300, work until 1600 when we knock off. If you in the liberty section, you free to put on you dress canvas and hit the beach. If you in the duty section and you ain't on a work detail, you get out of them work dungarees and shift into you undress blues. You cain't eat evening chow in dungarees unless you on a work detail. After chow when it dark they show a movie either on the mess deck or the fantail.

"One other thing. Linton don't go for no motherfuckin' transistor radios playin' down here. He usually playin' pinochle for money and he don't want to hear that shit you play.

"Okay, that it. Get in you dungarees and get topside for the fresh water washdown."

*   *   *

Liberty in Long Beach presented a range of options for a young bluejacket, not all of which were available for a baby-faced, 150 pound eighteen-year old only six months removed from boot camp. Like most Navy towns in the 'fifties, the main drag was lined with bars, tattoo parlors, jewelry stores and, of course the obligatory Christian Servicemen's Center which would offer sandwiches, soft drinks and counseling regarding the dens of iniquity where loose women and sailors would congregate to while away the hours in drink and whatever amorous adventure which might present itself. For Ken Walpole and myself there was the *Nu-Pike*.

The *Nu-Pike* was an amusement park located just behind the main drag and down three long tiers of cement steps. For me, the "Pike" was reminiscent of the boardwalks of the Jersey shore resorts, and offered various rides, a fun house (which was discovered to have an actual mummified corpse hanging from one of its beams), a twin track roller coaster, movie theater, dance palace, bars, and a sideshow replete with a human pin-cushion, sword swallower, fire eater, knife-thrower and hypno-tist. Stalls where games of "skill" offered kewpie dolls and the like to the lucky winner lined the promenade.

*   *   *

While I can't remember exactly where, I do recall reading some-where that everyone has a moment in their lifetime which will afford them fifteen minutes of fame. If that is the case then it doesn't surprise me that even my pinochle-playing, transis-tor-radio hating, hard-ass boss Linton would experience his in an all-to-familiar way. Linton had a set liberty plan from which he almost never deviated. He would depart the ship at 1600 on the Friday of his 72-hour weekend, grab a cab into Long Beach and begin to cruise the sailor bars which were lined up in a row on the main drag above the *Nu Pike*. His usual route was: Start at one end of the bars on the strip, and work his way eastward, visiting the *Cruiser, Midway and New York Grill* until he reached the last bar in the string, the *Saratoga Bar & Grill*. He would then find a cab, return to the ship and crawl into his bunk. The next day he'd get up around noon, shower, shave, head for the beach and retrace his steps from the previous evening, the only difference being that on Saturday he would begin his rounds in the early afternoon which, by the time the bars closed on Saturday night, the day's drinking left him carrying a serious package of booze soaking his brain, liver and kidneys.

On the Saturday night that Linton experienced his fifteen minutes, he exited the Saratoga Bar and Grill at closing time with enough alcohol in his system that could fell an elephant, staggered over to the concrete steps leading to the *Nu Pike* below and announced to all within earshot that he had downed enough beer to be able to…er…"piss" from the top to the very bottom of those steps without hitting any of the steps in between. A crowd of equally inebriated sailors gathered, anxious to witness first-hand this remarkable attempt. Wagers were placed, odds were negotiated, side bets on the number of steps that would be cleared were laid down. Cheers erupted from the onlookers while Linton unbuttoned the thirteen buttons that secured his trouser front, took position at the top of the steps and generated a truly *remarkable* stream of urine which targeted the very bottom of the concrete cascade.

Linton had the pressure behind the stream. He had the proper angle of attack. He had the wind at his back. It looked like he was going to make it!

Sadly, what Linton did not have was the acquiescence of the Shore Patrol and the Long Beach City Police, who arrived to investigate the ruckus, were not entertained, and proceeded to vigorously belabor Linton about the head, shoulders and other extremities before hauling his "drunk ass" off to the hoosegow.

Many have been called. Few have been chosen.

* * *

The Long Beach, California Nu-Pike

Captain Tuna

Winter, 1961

The skipper of my diesel-electric submarine was about to lower the boom. I was expecting the worst.

"Young man, would you care to tell your side of the story?"

'Yeah, like that's gonna make a difference,' I thought.

"Captain, all I can say is that there was a fight in a bar on the other side of the island and someone from the Brit submarine crew smashed a bottle over our cab driver's head. Larson and I had no way to get back to Hamilton before liberty expired."

Lieutenant-Commander Meyer nodded.

"What about the Bermudian police arresting the two of you for public urination?"

"That's on Larson, not me. He said he couldn't hold it any longer and walked over to the traffic kiosk in the middle of the street and pissed in it. I guess he thought it was a public urinal."

Meyer next addressed my division officer, Friar Tuck – well, his real name was Lieutenant jaygee Fred Smith – and invited him to offer any defense for me.

Good luck with that. Smith hated me and I him. He was an old submarine hand, a mustang who had worked his way up from enlisted electrician's mate and was the boat's first lieutenant. Fat, sarcastic, and with only a thin wisp of scraggily red hair occupying the perimeter which defended a bald pate, he and I knocked heads from the moment that I reported aboard the boat in the New Hampshire submarine shipyard.

"Captain, this young man has been a problem since he reported aboard in Portsmouth a year ago. He has consistently lagged in his submarine qualification training, has been a problem ashore both in Key West and our July 4th visit to Port Everglades. In my twenty-three years of submarine service I have never recommended that a shipmate be disqualified and sent to the surface navy, but in this man's case I have no alternative."

Meyer nodded again, paused and looked up from the charge sheet on his desk.

"Sailor, have you completed your qualification check for each system?"

I nodded in the affirmative. "Yes, sir. I'm waiting for the final walk-through exam."

Friar Tuck had one more nail to drive into my coffin.

"Not true, Captain. He has completed only six of the nine systems exams."

'You son-of-a-bitch.'

Meyer gave Smith a perplexed look.

"Mister Smith, this man says that he has completed all systems exams and is waiting for a final walk-through. You say he hasn't. Which is correct?"

I knew what was coming next. Old Friar Tuck had shit-canned my last three exams.

Smith produced the manila folder that he had brought to the discipline hearing and handed it to the captain.

"Here's his quals record, Captain."

Meyer took the folder, opened it, leafed through the documents and handed the folder back to Smith.

"What about it sailor? The paperwork has you three months shy after being aboard for more than a year."

I gave Friar Tuck a look of disgust. He was standing next to me looking like the cat who had caught the canary.

I shook my head. "Apparently my last three quals months have been thrown away. I suspect that Mister Smith, who threatened to punch my lights out shortly after I arrived, has conveniently made them unavailable."

Meyer didn't believe me, or perhaps he didn't want to believe my defense.

"I have seen and heard enough.

"Son, service in submarines means that every man aboard is his brother submariner's keeper. Should an engineering failure occur it is imperative that every man on board know enough about the boat and her operating systems to be able to step in and locate the casualty.

"You say that you have completed your qualifications. Your division officer, a man who has served his entire career in diesel-electric submarines, says that you have not.

"Based on the documentation in your quals record and your division officer's recommendation, I am recommending to

Submarine Squadron Six that you be transferred from the submarine service back to the surface fleet.

"As there is a possibility that an administrative error has occurred…

Meyer gave a cold look at Smith.

…I will do what I can to recommend that you be assigned to the type of ship that you request."

I nodded that I understood. I was damned if I would thank him for shit-canning me based on Friar Tuck's lie.

"I'd like to go back to the destroyer navy which was where I was before volunteering for submarines, Captain."

Meyer nodded.

"I will make the recommendation.

"Now, to wrap this up. For the incident involving the police in Hamilton you are reduced one grade. When we arrive in Norfolk you will report to Submarine Squadron Six to await orders. Your grade reduction is effective today for pay purposes. You may apply for reinstatement in three months if you keep your nose clean.

"Do you understand the results of this administrative mast?"

"Yes, sir."

"Very well. Dismissed.

"Mister Smith, I'd like a word with you before you leave."

*   *   *

After a near disaster during the submerged transit back to Norfolk from Bermuda when a weld on one of the engineering room salt water diesel cooling pipes failed and the ship plunged to near 1000 feet below her tested pressure depth before the crew managed to blow the filled ballast tanks with enough air to get us back to the surface, I was beginning to feel a little better about heading back to the "surface skimmer navy." Destroyer duty was sounding better and better to me when I reflected upon what could have happened to us had the engineers not closed the valve to that ruptured pipe. Lady luck had been riding on our collective shoulders that early morning. Once on the surface we limped back to Norfolk on the only serviceable diesel that would run, arriving a full 6 days later than expected.

Once we had tied up at the submarine pier in Norfolk I said goodbye to a few of my shipmate friends and proceeded to the *Subron Six* office at the end of the pier.

I entered the office, noticing that I was the only sailor in the room that wasn't wearing the submarine-qualified dolphins pinned to their jumpers. My arrival was anticipated.

"Well, son it says that you have been removed from the submarine service, and your captain asks that you be assigned to destroyer duty. That correct?"

"Yes sir, commander. I had been striking for the radarman rating on a destroyer before l left for submarine school."

"I see. Well where you go is out of our hands here as the Bureau of personnel in D.C. handles that. I suspect that Lieutenant Commander Meyer was trying to ease the bad news for you a bit."

'Shit. Get ready to take one in the shorts. They're going to send me to some screwed-up ship somewhere.'

The *Subron Six* officer continued.

"You have been reduced back to seaman apprentice and we have reviewed and approved the reduction.

"You'll be assigned a bunk over at the Naval Operating Base transient barracks. You will muster there each morning. If they have a work detail for you, you'll do it. If not, take the base shuttle back over here to see if we need anything from you administratively. If we do not you are free to go until the next day. Is that understood?"

'I've been shitcanned from submarines, I'm not stupid.'

"Yes sir, quite clear."

"Alright, then. I was going to ask what happened on the trip back from Bermuda, but I doubt that you have a clue."

"A salt-water cooling pipe weld failed and flooded the engine room before the chief on watch went under the flood water and secured the stop valve to the ruptured pipe. We blew all ballast tanks and stopped the descent at 1700 feet."

The commander nodded.

"Alright son, that's all."

I saluted, turned and said goodbye to the submarine service.

*   *   *

"Request permission to come aboard, sir."

The "destroyer" that Captain Meyer had mentioned at my mast had somehow morphed into the *USS Nantahala*, an aging, World War II vintage fleet oiler.

I saluted the flag which was flying from the in-port flag-staff on the fantail, turned and saluted the Officer of the Deck, who introduced himself as the operations officer, Lieutenant Noyes. Noyes retrieved my packet of service records and my orders, visually scanned the orders and handed them to the petty officer of the watch.

"Log this new sailor in the deck log and send for someone from ship's office to take charge of his records. I don't want them laying around the quarterdeck all night.

"Welcome aboard. I'm Lieutenant Noyes, the ship's operations officer. Where are you coming from?"

"Submarines, sir."

"Well then this is not your first ship. What did you do while in the submarine service?"

I presented my case to avoid the deck force.

"Nothing of any use here, sir, but before submarines I was a CIC watchstander in a fast tin can on the west coast. I have over 15 months of standing watches in CIC, as well as the duties of in-port watchstanding and other ship's functions. In fact, I have already completed the courses for Radarman 3 & 2, as well as military requirements for petty officer 3 & 2, and have completed a six-week course in CIC watchstanding at Treasure Island.

"I did have a bit of a setback, but that was just temporary. I think I will be able to cut it here in your CIC."

Mister Noyes thought for a moment.

"Well, possession is nine points of the law and we are short-handed in CIC. How would you like to be a part of Operations Department as a CIC watchstander?"

'Yesss!'

"Nothing would suit me better, sir."

"Good answer. You are now a part of the Operations Department, OI Division. Your lead petty officer is Radarman Second Dave Julius. He's a married man and not aboard tonight so we'll get the duty ops petty officer up here to assign you a bunk in the forward superstructure.

"I'll clear all this with the XO first thing in the morning before our bos'un gets wind of it."

*   *   *

By May of 1961 I had gotten my seaman stripes back and we were in the early stages of a six-month deployment to the Sixth Fleet in the Mediterranean Sea. Our main task was fighting boredom interspersed with times of intense activity when a carrier task group of destroyers and the aircraft carrier that the accompanying "small boy" destroyers were designed to protect would appear on the horizon to refuel and receive the limited amount of fuel, cargo, fresh vegetables and mail that we would have aboard for them. *Nantahala* was also the clearing house for movies that the other ships would show for their crews: They would send over by highline the movies that had been viewed by the task group and we would send over a fresh batch of films that the ships in the task group had presumably not seen.

When I referred to intense activity I meant intense activity for everyone on the ship except OI Division. The operational doctrine of the day was that radar emissions during refueling presented a potential danger for fuel ignition - think of the cell phone warnings around today's gas pumps - and when the bos'un of the watch passed the word to extinguish the smoking lamp throughout the ship he also passed the word to secure all electronic equipment. That meant that the watch supervisor would go into the radar transmitter room in the back of CIC and shut down our lone search radar, leaving us with nothing to do for the six to eight hour refueling operation.

Our commanding officer aboard *Nantahala* was Captain Arthur F. Johnson, a naval officer who had spent his entire at sea career as a destroyer man. Rumor had it that if Captain Johnson could survive one year as skipper of a deep draft vessel such as ours he was in line to be promoted to commodore and lead a squadron of destroyers.

Johnson was a large man, about six-foot four and weighing around 220 pounds, a nervous, nitpicking, prudish micro-manager who was constantly reviewing the current operational order to see which officers of ships that we were replenishing were senior to him and which were junior. He was constantly worried about protocol and drove the XO, Lieutenant Commander Norton and all the ship's department heads nutty carrying out silly, niggling orders so that any senior officer or foreign dignitary who may visit the ship wouldn't take offense, as if anyone would care to visit a broken down old World War II oiler. The officers and crew began calling him "Captain Tuna."

* * *

The *Saratoga* and her screening destroyers had completed the refueling and re-arming from us and were dancing briskly toward the horizon, headed for some exotic Mediterranean port-of-call. We were riding high in the water, having expended our cargo of black oil, aviation fuel, ammunition, mail and movies during the replenishment operation.

Chick Ciolino, who was standing the 1200 to 1600 boatswain's mate of the watch on the bridge, popped his head into CIC which was located directly behind the bridge and connected by a door.

"Hey man, where we headed now? Cannes, Istanbul, where we going to next?"

I smiled. "Hate to disappoint you, Chick, but we are headed to Pozzouli and the fueling pier to take on black oil for the next at-sea period. After that, it's beautiful downtown Naples, the asshole of the Mediterranean."

"Ah shit. Hate that place. Everybody thinks I've got it made just because I'm Italian. Hell, I'm from Chicago, can't even *speak* Eye-talian."

Pozzuoli was located at the extreme western end of the Gulf of Naples and had gained a modicum of fame as the birthplace of Sophia Loren. From my vantage point I could see little else to recommend it. We would remain there only long enough to top off all our fuel tanks. From there we would be back underway to provide fueling service for the ships in the fleet that were operating at sea.

Maneuvering a large single screw oiler up to the fueling pier was tricky business usually requiring three tugboats: one pushing the bow, one astern and one standing by to push wherever the harbor pilot directed. While the harbor pilot would give the orders to the tugs it was still the Captain who held overall responsibility for the safe docking and undocking of the ship. These dockings usually set old Captain "Tuna" in an absolute frenzy of worry. He would dash from one bridge wing to the other, wringing his hands and peppering the pilot with questions whose answers were designed to ease some of the Captain's worry about the docking process. It was all one could do to keep from laughing out loud.

It was on this voyage to the fuel piers that Chick Ciolino uttered the line that made him famous - at least to those of us who were close enough to hear it.

As we made the initial approach to Pozzouli, the Captain had the word passed to set the Special Sea and Anchor Detail which was done to provide the ship with the most experienced people to conduct the close in docking maneuver. My Sea Detail station was as the Captain's special sound powered phone talker that established a communication line directly between CIC and the Captain. While in the Gulf we would provide a steady stream of information on the radar contacts of close by sea craft and make recommendations on course maneuvers from our navigation plot. As we got closer to the fuel pier, the Captain would have me pass the word to CIC to secure the ship's radar. For the rest of the docking I would become just an observer as CIC had no information to pass along to the bridge.

Captain Tuna was in an absolute state of distress by this time. He had trouble understanding - or perhaps trusting - the Italian pilot maneuvering the ship. Finally, he could stand it no longer. The pilot had just used his bullhorn to direct the bow tug to stand off while the stern tug pushed the ship's fantail closer to the pier.

Captain Tuna was, as usual, a nervous wreck gesturing wildly to the tug, which was ignoring the Captain and awaiting the harbor pilot's next command.

"No, no, no! Keep that tug on the bow pushing! Keep the bow tug pushing! We are not going to get number one line to the pier. Push forward! Forward!"

The pilot threw up his hands in disgust and began hurling a stream of invective in Italian at the Captain. One could only imagine what the outburst meant.

The Captain turned and called out to his other phone talker, Chick Ciolino.

"Ciolino, you're Italian," Captain Tuna said in what today would be a most politically incorrect utterance. "Tell that tug forward to get back on the bow and resume pushing."

"But Captain, I'm..." Ciolino began.

"Dammit Ciolino, tell that tug forward to get back on the bow and resume pushing."

Ciolino Shrugged.

"Aye aye, Captain," Ciolino acknowledged.

Ciolino walked over to the side of the bridge wing, put two fingers to his lips, gave a loud, shrill whistle and pointed to the bow.

"Hey! Joe! Pusha-a da sheep!"

Captain Tuna, the chicken of the sea.

*   *   *

Diesel-electric submarine Barbel

Fleet Oiler Nantahala

The World-Famous Jet Inn

Spring, 1964

Wake up, shipmate. Get out of your rack and get dressed. Come on, man. Wake the fuck up."

I rolled over and opened one eye to see why Geno was shaking my shoulder.

"Shit! What time is it Geno? What's going on? The barracks on fire?"

I opened the other eye to get a better look at Geno and took a deep breath, exhaling as I swung down from my top bunk and slipped into my flip-flops. He was dressed in his civvies, short-sleeved sport shirt, slacks and boat shoes with no socks. He was obviously in a hurry to leave the reconnaissance wing base and go into Sanford.

"Zero-eight-thirty, shipmate. It's Saturday, I ain't got duty and I'm heavy on the hip. We need to make breakfast at the Jet.

"Somebody got to read the funny papers to Chuck. He's the day bartender today."

I was still in the process of clearing the cobwebs from my brain. I took a second cleansing breath.

"Geno, I just left Sarah's house at five this morning. I am not only tired, but I'm dead broke, low on gas for the Triumph and payday is a week away. I can't go anywhere."

Geno reached in his pocket and pulled out a wad of twenty-dollar bills.

"You don't need any money, my very good shipmate. I just harpooned the base credit union yesterday for a signature loan."

He peeled five twenties from his bankroll and handed them to me.

"Told you I was heavy on the hip, shipmate. That's for you to play with. You got the wheels and I got the cash. Get dressed and let's ride."

Aviation Structural Mechanic Second Class Irby Gene Lunn, short, muscular, tough and hyper-energetic, grew up on the mean streets of the Baltimore suburb of Highland Town. He learned to use his fists at a very early age and it was from those early days fighting for survival in Baltimore City that he earned a reputation as one mean-assed dude. You didn't mess with Geno. If you did, you were liable to end up in the emergency room.

Geno joined the Navy at seventeen and instantly found a home. He knew the airframe of the supersonic Vigilante carrier-based reconnaissance aircraft better than anyone in the training squadron and when on duty was an absolute dynamo on the flight line. He seemed to be everywhere at once, performing maintenance quality checks and working on structural problems. His maintenance department chief viewed him as a go-to guy whenever a problem with the aircraft presented itself. Geno loved being an airframe mechanic and was a hard worker. When off-duty he played every bit as hard as he worked - if not harder.

We were as different as night and day, Geno and me. I had arrived at the Navy recon air base eight months earlier from the forward-deployed carrier *Shangri-La* via two months of school at the North American Aviation aircraft manufacturing plant in Columbus, Ohio for a two-year tour as an instructor at the new *Integrated Operational Intelligence Center (IOIC)*. Geno had been attached to the training squadron for the past two years and was due to deploy with one of the operational squadrons in late summer of 1965, the following year. Geno's job was to assist in keeping his squadron's aircraft flying. Mine was to train the air intelligence sailors on the detection and location of the missile and anti-aircraft emplacements of the enemy in the airspace over North Vietnam and any other hot spot where the ship was operating.

Geno and I did have a couple of things in common. We both loved to "run the roads," as he put it and chase the women who frequented the honky-tonks in the three county Central Florida area where we were stationed. Lord knows that there were plenty of young women living in and around Sanford, Florida during the mid-sixties and they all seemed to have taken a liking to the sailors from the recon base.

There was one other thing that we both shared: an emerging drinking problem. Geno would pay for his with his life before the decade had finished. I was more fortunate. I was only reduced in rank by two pay grades.

*   *   *

I pulled the Triumph TR-3 into the dirt and gravel parking lot in front of the run-down and dilapidated World-Famous Jet Inn and killed the ignition. We exited the car and walked into the bar. It was empty except for the bartender, Chuck Polite.

Polite had recently been discharged from the Navy on less than desirable terms when it was discovered that he had more than one wife. This fact in and of itself was certainly not grounds for being reduced one rank and shown the way to the main gate except that his marital timeline was not quite kosher. It seems that Chuck had two wives simultaneously, an annoying detail which was enough for Uncle Sam to unceremoniously sack him. Seventeen years as a navy ship's cook went cascading down the floor drain.

The smell of stale beer and cigarettes permeated the bar. Geno and I sat at the bar next to the drive-through window.

"Geno and Nasty. Hell of a way to start my shift. What'll it be?"

We both laid a twenty on the bar and Gino ordered our "breakfast."

"Couple of drafts, shipmate, and a shot of Popov vodka. Let's have some of those pickled eggs and sausage with it. Gotta have some food in the stomach. Got a pocketful of money and the day is just gettin' started."

I decided to modify my order.

"Chuck, make mine a shot of Bacardi Light."

Polite nodded, reached for the rum bottle and deftly poured a full shot into a large shot glass.

I reached into my pocket and pulled out a roll of Tums. Geno looked at me and smiled.

"They better be industrial strength, shipmate. When we're done here I'm thinkin' that we need to spend some time at the Caribe Lounge downtown."

I took a deep breath, threw back the Bacardi, shuddered, and chased it with a swig from the draft beer mug that had been placed in front of me.

Chuck Polite shook his head and snorted derisively.

"If you two keep this up you won't make two o'clock happy-hour."

Geno laughed.

"Well, we could drive over to Sunland Estates and watch the sailors who were shacked up with the Heavy Seven wives pack and leave before the squadron returns from the Mediterranean cruise Monday.

"What about you, Nasty? You got anything needs to go from Sarah's house?"

I shook my head.

"Sarah is separated from her husband and has filed for divorce, but to answer your question, all I had over there was a toothbrush and I shit-canned it just in case.

"From what Sarah tells me, Tex is not too keen on getting a divorce. I thought I'd better move back into the barracks just to prevent any... unpleasantness."

It was Chuck's turn to laugh.

"Unpleasantness my ass, you just don't want to get shot. I'm betting that he's going to be looking for you anyway. Ain't no secrets that stay secret for long in Sunland Estates."

"I'll cross that bridge when I come to it, Chuck. Between now and then I'll..."

The sound of a car pulling into the gravel driveway interrupted the conversation. The door to the World-Famous Jet Inn opened and newly promoted Chief Bruce Hodge walked in.

Geno was the first to greet him.

"Well if it ain't the teenage Chief himself. How ya doin' Chief?"

Hodge smiled.

"Hello, Geno, Nasty. Chuck, how about a Jack and Coke for a thirsty guy who has been working all night?"

Twenty-four-year-old Bruce Hodge and I had trained together in Columbus at the North American Aviation plant on the new Integrated Operational Intelligence Center and had pulled a few liberties together in that college town. He was the supervisor in the Univac computer room that analyzed incoming intelligence tapes from the aircraft electronic "sniffers" and converted the raw data into usable tactical intelligence. Hodge had been selected for promotion to chief petty officer in the minimum time possible – seven years and nine months. Before he "put the hat on" as a chief petty officer I had always called him "Bruce" and he had always addressed me by either my given or surname, depending on the circumstances. Now that Hodge had made chief I decided that my communication with him while on liberty would remain as "Bruce" but while on duty in the working environment it would always be "Chief."

That's how it *is* in the Navy.

Hodge drained the cocktail in two gulps and handed the empty glass back to Chuck.

"One for the other leg, Chuck, then I'm going home and crash. I am beat."

Something was up, and I wanted to know exactly what it was.

"Bruce, this working all night business, I never got the word that we were going to work the night through. What's going on?"

Hodge paused for a moment, then decided that there was no classified information that could be divulged if he answered.

"Your branch wasn't involved. Storage and Retrieval got a new order-of-battle for China, North Vietnam and the Soviets yesterday afternoon. We usually just get updates but this time it was the whole magilla. Case after case of IBM punch cards arrived under the control of an armed courier. Chief Martinez and Miles Underwood began running them through the collator to my main frame over in Data Processing. I told the married pukes to go on home and I stayed all night to make sure we got the new data written on mag tape.

"Put that together with the OPNAV message that arrived in personnel yesterday and it looks like something big is about to happen."

Geno and I exchanged glances.

"What OPNAV message are you talking about, Bruce? I haven't seen any."

Hodge nodded.

"Personnel got it yesterday. The Navy is calling for volunteers to serve one-year tours in-country Vietnam. All rates and all specialties. They are looking for supply and logistic types, administration and aviation specialties, deck rates for river warfare and advisory duty, the whole shebang. They are offering one-grade after tour meritorious promotions, monthly hostile fire bonuses and tax-free pay for the whole time in-country."

Geno turned and looked at me. I could see the wheels turning inside his head.

"Ain't no quicker way to promotion, shipmates. And with extra pay in the bargain.

"I'll be headed for personnel Monday to volunteer. What about you, shipmate?"

I thought about it for a moment.

"Why not? I'll go with you and volunteer as well."

Polite gave a derisive snort.

"If you two are goin' over there I'm gonna see about buyin' North Veet-nam war bonds. Haw!"

Bruce Hodge threw down the second Jack and Coke and got up from the bar stool.

"See you road-runners later. I'm headed for the barn."

After Bruce Hodge left we sat at the bar for a few hours while Chuck gave us the blow-by-blow of his upcoming move up to Batavia, New York to embark on a career of piloting an over-the-road 18-wheeler truck.

"What about Ellie and the kids?"

Ellie was Chuck's new wife. The kids, all six of them, were thought to belong to her ex-husband, a bombardier-navigator from one of the Skywarrior squadrons.

"Yep, part and parcel. They're coming too and so is the child support."

"Good God almighty, shipmate! You gonna drive all the way to New York with Ellie, her kids and all that furniture?

"You gonna need one of them 18-wheelers to move all that shit."

"Furniture belongs to the ex-husband as does the house. Just me, Ellie and the kids are goin'."

"Well," Geno replied, "If you ain't headed up north right now how 'bout pouring us another round?

*   *   *

After a few hours of conversation about nothing in particular and listening to Geno's predictions regarding the state of the current Baltimore Orioles' chances for a pennant, Chuck asked if I would watch the bar as he had to "take a shit."

"That's too much information, Chuck, but yes, I'll tend the bar while you are in the men's room."

"Well, here's the thing, the men's room is dirty, so I'll be using the ladies' room. It ain't so bad in there. If a woman comes in and wants to use the can tell her it's out of order and we're waiting for a plumber."

Geno and I exchanged knowing glances.

"I think I can remember that, Chuck. Go do your thing."

Chuck and I exchanged places behind the bar and he headed around the corner for the ladies' room to do his business.

It was almost as if the whole event had been scripted. Except for Bruce Hodge's brief visit Geno and I had been the only customers in the saloon all morning. Just moments after Chuck had entered the ladies' room we heard a car pulling into the driveway.

Geno grinned. "Nasty, are you thinking what I'm thinking?"

I smiled back. "Oh yeah."

Cue the bathroom scene.

A woman entered the bar obviously in distress.

"Sir, may I please use your ladies' room? I can't wait much longer."

Geno and I exchanged an evil glance.

"Why certainly, ma'am," I answered, "right around the corner, first door to your left."

We waited for it. Five…, four…, three…, two…, one…,

"Shriek!"

"Whoa! Goddamn you, Nasty!"

The woman, who had been in the early stages of preparation to use the loo came running for the door while adjusting her shorts. Chuck followed shortly thereafter, hopping around with one pantleg in place and the other helplessly dragging along the floor.

"You son-of-a-bitch. You said you were gonna tell her that the ladies' was out of order."

I was laughing so hard I could hardly reply: "I didn't say that. I said that I thought I could remember your request."

Geno and I gathered our change from the bar, left Chuck a tip and exited the World-Famous Jet Inn headed for downtown and a few drinks at the Caribe Lounge, leaving Chuck struggling with his trousers.

*   *   *

That evening, after a bit of a rest and a shower we arrived back at the World-Famous Jet Inn. I'll tell you this much about Saturdays at the Jet: if you can't hook up at the Jet on Saturday night you may as well consider becoming a priest. Women from the surrounding towns were always at the Jet on Saturday nights. Sarah told me that the women called it "sailor-shopping."

Maxine, Geno's girlfriend was already there and waiting for us. A waitress at Freddie's Steak house in Maitland, Maxine was thirty-five or so, very attractive and was a party girl. She had brought her sister Muriel with her, ostensibly to meet me but that wasn't happening as Sarah and I were to meet later that evening for one last tryst before soon-to-be-divorced husband Tex returned. I wasn't about to miss that last evening together for Muriel, a forty-ish, slightly overweight older sister whose style of fashion was to wear fake bluebirds in her hair. Fake bluebirds!

The three of us, Geno, Maxine and I took a seat at the bar. Muriel, realizing that I was not going to be her date, was busily engaged chatting with Solly, a sailor more her age. They took an open booth and seemed to be getting along quite nicely.

The first round was mine; Max ordered a Tom Collins, Geno a vodka and club soda. My preference for the evening was a Bacardi and Coke. The jukebox was blaring a Buck Owens tune, "My Heart Skips a Beat," and everyone was having a great Saturday evening. When the jukebox stopped playing, Prune-Face Annie, the fifty-ish cocktail waitress who had spent much too much time in the sun as a young woman, would screech at the top of her lungs, "Sure is quiet in here," and collect quarters for the jukebox. The sound of her voice was very close to the sound of rubbing two pieces of sandpaper together in front of a microphone thanks to her two-pack of Camel cigarettes a day habit.

It was, quite simply, great to be alive that Saturday night! I was waiting for the results of a promotional exam that would advance me to 1st class petty officer, I was having a few drinks with friends in a Central Florida town and was soon to meet up with my girl Sarah, whose love-making would cause "a bull-dog to hug a hound," to quote a lyric from a Clark Terry-Bob Brookmeyer song.

We were into our third round of drinks – Max insisted on buying when it was her turn, the sweetheart – when an over-the-road trucker whose name I would later learn was Neil walked in and stood directly behind Max and Geno. Max cast a nervous glance in his direction.

"What the fuck, Max you alone or you with fat boy here?"

'Here we go.'

I had seen it before. I knew what was coming.

Max tried to defuse the encounter. I knew that it was already too late for that.

"Neil, you and I have been split for six months. It is over, we both know that."

"It's over when I say it's over, whore. Now get your ass up and let's go."

He never saw it coming. In one lightning move Geno leaped from his stool, gave a half-turn to the right, planted his feet and delivered a crushing left to the trucker's jaw. Neil fell back, hit the wall and sat unceremoniously with his back to the wall and ass on the concrete floor, spitting blood and teeth.

Geno ran over to the dazed trucker, pulled him up by the front of his t-shirt and punched him repeatedly in the face.

Neil began to wave his right hand feebly, a signal that he was done before he even started.

"You bother her again and I'll *really* hurt you. You understand, asshole?"

The trucker wobbled his battered head in what appeared to be a sign that he understood.

"Now, motherfucker, tell her your sorry."

The trucker coughed and spit blood and broken teeth on the barroom floor.

"Sorry."

Dawn, the night bartender came over to me and spoke in a low voice.

"Someone called 911 on the pay phone. Get out of here before the cops come."

I nodded and walked over to Geno and Max.

"Cops are coming. Best to get underway. Now."

Geno stood up, gathered Max, Muriel and Solly. The four headed for the parking lot and Max's Pontiac.

I leaned over the trucker and helped him to a booth.

"Cops are coming and probably an ambulance. Do you know who that was that hit you?"

"No."

"Good. And the girl he was with?"

"Yeah. Max."

"Not good. Can you forget who she is, or do you want "Fat Boy" to come after you?"

"Oh. Okay. No, I don't know her."

Good. Keep it like that. I'll buy you a drink next time I see you.

I turned and left. I had to meet Sarah at the Trophy Lounge.

*   *   *

"Hi, honey, you're a little late. Where were you?"

"Hi. I was at the Jet having a drink with Geno."

She smiled. "Oh. How is everyone at the Jet?'

I gave her a big grin.

"You know. Just another Saturday night at the World-Famous Jet Inn."

*   *   *

A3B training aircraft and RA-5C reconnaissance aircraft

Semper Fi

Autumn, 1967

We were all tired. USS Constellation was on the verge of completing her third seven-month combat cruise in the South China Sea in less than three years. Flying into the enemy's home turf which was teeming with anti-aircraft guns and missile sites, launching strike and reconnaissance missions every ninety minutes, twelve hours a day, seven days a week for thirty days or more at a clip before being allowed one full day to "stand down" had taken a toll on the maintenance and support crews as well as the pilots themselves, who were becoming a bit skittish about launching and flying into the vicious maelstrom that was North Vietnam's anti-aircraft environment.

*   *   *

The current thirty-day combat period was to be our last before we "out-chopped" to head for San Diego after a brief stop in Subic Bay and Pearl Harbor, and the entire crew of support sailors and air wing pilots were more than ready to depart for home after losing sixteen aircraft and twenty crew that had been either killed or captured.

I was tired as well. I was a designated "Yankee Team" asset, hopping from carrier to carrier as one ship finished their combat tour and was replaced by a fresh carrier and air wing.

Please don't misunderstand. I liked the job I was doing, and the extra tax-free hostile fire pay was nice to have when we pulled into one of the ports in Japan or the Philippines, Hong Kong or Australia for R&R. Yankee Team asset personnel were strictly volunteers. I had raised my hand when the call came and as a result I'd been bouncing around "cross-decking" since late 1965, running the electronic evaluation area of the ship's integrated photo and electronic intelligence center as well as de-briefing our crews that flew electronic recon missions. "Unarmed and Unafraid" was the recon squadron's unofficial motto.

"Yeah, right," was the unofficial response from the crews that flew those missions.

We were headed stateside in two weeks and I was going with them. When the call for cross-deck volunteers comes out this time I'm keeping my damn hands in my pockets! It was time to take some leave when we got back to San Diego and head back east for Christmas with my family.

* * *

"Boss wants to see you in his office out front."

"Roger that." I exited the air lock that separated the admin area from the evaluation and processing area, walked over to Lieutenant-Commander Mecaughey's office and tapped lightly on the bulkhead before entering.

"Want to see me, sir?"

"I did. Come in, Bob and have a seat."

'Uh oh, something's up. What the hell's he got in store for me?'

"Thank you, sir. What's up?"

"Your request for thirty-days leave when we get back to San Diego hit my desk this morning.

"I'm afraid that I'm going to have to turn it down. Seems like you have a set of orders and we've got to fly you out of here tomorrow on the mail plane headed for Subic."

"Sir, I'm afraid that I don't understand. Where would I be going that I have to get there in such a rush?"

Mecaughey picked up a naval message and handed it to me.

"Arrived at personnel this morning. You're going back to the Coronado Amphib Base for counterinsurgency training. When you finish there, you're headed in-country to pick up one of those new patrol gunboats at Da Nang."

'Shit. The Vietnam volunteer duty from Sanford when Geno and I volunteered back in '64.'

"I was under the impression that my volunteering for Yankee Team Asset duty took care of the volunteer chit that I signed back in Sanford."

Mecaughey shrugged. "Doesn't look like it, does it?

"Anyway, pack your seabag and report to Air Ops on the flight deck tomorrow morning at 0700. They have a seat for you on the mail plane. Personnel will have your formal orders, instructions and records ready for you to pick up by 1400 this afternoon.

"Your orders will tell you what you should do once you arrive at Subic. Good luck, sailor. We hate to lose you."

I was in a state of mild shock. I just nodded to the boss and left his office.

*　*　*

"We have a seat for you aboard an Air Force Starlifter next Thursday from Clark AFB over in Angeles City. Cubi Point has a twice-a-week afternoon hop from Cubi to Clark AFB with the C-45 Beechcraft. That will get you over there in time for the Starlifter hop.

"The Starlifter run to the States is a night hop. First stop is Elmendorf in Alaska for fuel, then on to Travis in California. We'll cut you a travel voucher to get from San Francisco down to San Diego. You can grab public transportation over to Coronado from there.

"Until then, I am assigning you to the Shore Patrol Headquarters which is the building just inside the gate. You'll be with them for the next seven days until your flight leaves. In case there is a seat cancellation at an earlier date you'll have to be ready to go when we call you. Understood?"

'Damn! I could have come back with the ship if I knew I'd be waiting around this long for the hop to the States.'

"Got it, Chief."

"Right. Get a bunk in the first-class quarters in the transient barracks, then report to Senior Chief Harper at Shore Patrol Headquarters."

*　*　*

Senior Chief Gunners Mate John "I.W." Harper – the "I.W." nickname represented his above average fondness for a certain brand of bourbon – was at his desk reviewing a few old arrest reports when I entered the Shore Patrol Headquarters.

"'Morning sailor. What can I do for you?"

"'Morning Chief. Base Admin sent me here for a temporary assignment until my flight stateside from Clark AFB is set to leave."

Harper nodded. "Well, they didn't say anything about it to me. What I really need is a third-class yeoman to handle all this fucking paperwork that you see on my desk, not a first-class radar scope dope.

"Can you type, by any chance?"

I smiled, shaking my head.

"Not a stroke, Chief. Sorry."

"Well, that's that. Tell you what, have you had breakfast yet?"

"No, Chief, can't say that I have."

Harper nodded.

"Well what say you take the pickup over to the geedunk and grab us a couple of bacon and egg sandwiches? We've got coffee here.

"I'll buy, you fly. That okay with you?"

This week with Chief Harper was shaping up to be a good one. I gave him a wide grin.

"Sounds Like a plan to me," I replied.

Harper swiveled his desk chair 180 degrees, opened the door to the gear locker and removed a navy-blue arm band with the letters "SP" printed in large yellow letters and a white web belt with attached billy-club and sheath.

"You know the drill, arm band around the upper right sleeve, billy-club hung from your right side, unless you are left-handed, then hang it on the left."

'Been there, done that.'

"Got it, Chief."

Harper retrieved his wallet and extracted a twenty-dollar bill.

"Don't have anything smaller now. Take the keys hanging on the vehicle key board marked "pickup". Know where the Exchange geedunk is?"

I gave a shrug. "I'll find it."

"Right. The arm band and billy-club will get you front-of-the-line service at the geedunk. Don't let anyone hold you up over there."

I gave Harper a 'thumbs-up, grabbed the keys to the pickup and left.

*   *   *

The time for the trip to the geedunk and back took only a half-hour. I entered the office with the bag of sandwiches, handed one bacon-and-egger to the chief, gave him his change and took a seat at the vacant yeoman desk.

"Alright, Scope-Dope. Appreciate the sandwich run."

Apparently, I'd been given a new nickname for the time that I'd be working for Harper. I didn't mind. I knew that old school sailors only handed them out to those they liked.

We were in the process of unwrapping the sandwiches when the patrol panel truck pulled up, followed by an Olongapo City Police jeep. Two city policemen were in the jeep's front seat. A middle-aged Filipino man was riding on the back bench.

The first-class electrician's mate who was driving the panel truck turned off the motor, exited the vehicle, walked around to the two rear panel doors and opened them. Two bedraggled-looking, handcuffed Marines stumbled from the truck's rear, squinting in the morning sunlight. The first-class electrician motioned for the two Marines to go inside Shore Patrol Headquarters. The Marines stumbled through the glass double doors and stood in front of Chief Harper's desk. The two policemen and the civilian followed with the driver of the shore patrol van.

Chief Harper was the first to speak. He addressed the shore patrolman who was driving the van, a first-class petty officer by the name of Williamson.

"What have you got here, Willie?"

Williamson pointed to one of the two Marines.

"Couple of young Marines here, Chief. They got into a fight with the manager at the Utopia Club over a girl who they say robbed this one here and they busted up some furniture, the manager and the girl.

"City police were the first to show up and the Marine snuffys got into a scrape with them as well. Cops finally got 'em handcuffed and hauled 'em off to the local slammer. I picked 'em up this morning on the morning jail sweep."

Harper took a bite of his sandwich and nodded.

"Okay so far, but what are the two city cops and the civilian doing with you?"

The civilian Filipino began to speak loudly in his native Tagalog. One of the city policemen slapped the man on the side of his head, indicating that the man should shut up.

Williamson continued his account of the previous evening's altercation.

"The civilian is the manager of the Utopia Club. He's claiming monetary damages for the busted-up furniture and for medical treatment for himself and the girl."

Harper remained silent for a minute or so, swiveling from side to side in his desk chair.

"Medical treatment? Looks to me that he has a black eye and nothing more. And he wants money for a doctor?"

Williamson nodded. "That's right, Chief."

Chief Harper next questioned the Marines.

"Which of you two snuffys is the senior Marine?"

One man nodded his head, indicating that he was senior. "I am, Chief. Lance Corporal Crank, Chief."

"Well now, Lance Corporal Crank it appears to me that this 140-pound bar manager has gotten the better of the two of you. He don't look near as banged up as the two of you.

"He do all that damage to the two of you, did he?"

Lance Corporal Crank gave a sideway gesture with his head to indicate that it was the police that had worked the two over once they were in custody.

"I see. And the two of you were scrapping with the cops when my people arrived at the Utopia Club?"

Lance Corporal Crank nodded.

"Well then you two got what you deserved there. How much money did this one girl take and how did it happen that she was able to relieve you of it?"

The second Marine answered.

"Ninety-five dollars U.S., Chief. The money was in my wallet."

"Ninety-five dollars. Just how was she able to get your wallet without you knowing about it?"

The second Marine cleared his throat.

"Hum-hum. Well, you see Chief, the one girl was kind of giving me a massage under the table and this other girl distracted me. When I leaned over to kiss the other one she got my wallet and took the money."

Chief Harper shook his head and laughed. "Man, that must have been some *massage* you had going there. What happened after that?"

Lance Corporal Crank replied.

"We were pretty drunk, Chief, and we decided to go back to our outfit. We were almost to the main gate when my buddy checked his wallet and saw that he'd been robbed."

Chief Harper nodded and turned to the second Marine.

"You would be Lance Corporal Crank's 'buddy' I take it. What is your name?"

The second Marine nodded.

"Private First-Class Brown, Chief."

"Alright Brown, you checked your wallet and discovered the missing money. Then what?"

"Well Chief, I told my buddy here that I thought I felt something at the back of my pants while the one girl was giving me a hand...er...massage and that I thought that the other girl took my money from my wallet then."

Harper shook his head.

"You *thought* that you felt something? Why didn't you do something then?"

The young Marine blushed.

"Well, um, Chief it was kind of a bad time to stop what was going on, you know, and anyway I wasn't really sure."

Harper had heard enough.

"Alright.

"Willie, take these two Marines, uncuff 'em and put 'em in the holding cell in the back. We'll get 'em back to their battalion staging camp in the mountains later today."

As the two Marines left for the holding cell the Filipino civilian began waving his arms and speaking loudly in Tagalog to the two policemen.

Harper banged his fist sharply on his desk.

"QUIET, GODDAMMIT!"

Harper addressed the Filipino civilian.

"You are the manager of the Utopia Club?"

The Filipino nodded.

"How much money do you want for damages?"

The club manager thought for a moment.

"Three hundred dollars U.S. My club is ruined, I am hurt, and my girl cannot work as she has a broken nose."

Harper nodded.

"Alright, I will submit the paperwork to reimburse you. It will take a month or two to get this approved and there is the allegation of robbery that must be investigated which will, if thoroughly investigated and documented, will take a month or more.

"In the meantime, I am placing the Utopia Club "Off Limits" to all military personnel. No military man or woman will be allowed to patronize the Utopia club while the investigation proceeds. I will have one of my shore patrolmen placed at the entrance to enforce this."

The club manager began to protest.

"You cannot do dis. My club will be out of business. I will lose my job. Oh, Lord, Oh Lord, please Chief do not do dis. Oh Lord, oh Lord."

Harper nodded and motioned for the man to be silent.

"Well there *is* a way we can resolve this without shutting down your club."

The Filipino manager had been checkmated.

"What 'way' is dat?"

"You drop all charges and claims against the Navy and pay the police for their assistance and I will allow your club to remain open."

The manager nodded.

"What about de investigation?"

Harper replied.

"The investigation into the robbery goes away.... for now. Any further accusations of your people rolling my sailors and Marines and we shut you down for good.

"Agreed?"

The club manager shrugged.

"I hab no choice but to agree."

"Good. Now clear the hell out of here so I can finish my damn sandwich."

The Olongapo policemen and the club manager exited shore patrol headquarters and headed toward the main gate.

I was impressed. Chief Harper had defused the situation while potentially saving the Navy hundreds of dollars – or more – in damage costs.

"Chief, you really handled that situation well. That manager could have caused a lot of trouble. I had no idea that you had the authority to put the Utopia Club off limits to military personnel."

Chief Harper grinned.

"I don't. Only my boss, Commander Nash can authorize that, and only after he runs it by the base commander. That won't be a problem, Nash is an old boatswain's mate mustang. If he hears about it, he won't care."

Williamson returned from locking up the two young Marines in a holding cell.

"Willie, take our new arrival here with you on your afternoon rounds. When the ship shore patrolmen arrive, you and the new guy take 'em to their posts in town and show 'em where their posts start and end. We'll need to cull six of the ship guys to ride cattle car patrols for taking the drunks back to their commands at midnight when liberty expires."

"Scope Dope, when Willie finishes with you I want you to take the two snuffys in the holding cell back to their battalion. We use a mini-bus and have a local driver that knows where they are bivouacked. Take the two Marines and the arrest reports and turn them over to the duty NCO at battalion headquarters."

"Roger that, Chief."

Harper nodded. "Alright, Willie, saddle up and the two of you head out amongst 'em."

*　*　*

By the time Willie and I had made the patrol route rounds, briefed the sailors riding cattle car duty and gotten chow for the two Marines the clock had crept around to 1800. Chief Harper had left for the day and Willie had assumed the duty of senior shore patrol at the station until the overnight relief, a first-class equipment operator Seabee by the name of Ryan arrived.

I unlocked the holding cell, gathered the two young Marines, put them on the mini-bus and grabbed the arrest reports.

The driver started up the bus and headed for the mountains which enclosed the naval air station at Cubi Point. We exited the security gate and began our ascent, headed for the tent city that housed the Marine replacement battalion which was awaiting transport to Da Nang. After a ten-minute climb along a rutted and twisting road we arrived at the Marine battalion headquarters. I instructed the two Marines to wait in the bus while I went in to see the Duty NCO, who turned out to hold the rank of gunnery, or "gunny" sergeant.

"Evening Gunny. I've got two of yours that had a bit of trouble in town last night."

I handed the arrest reports to the gunny, who briefly scanned them and handed them back to me. We both exited the HQ tent and walked to the mini-bus.

The two young Marines weren't very anxious to leave the relatively safe confines of the mini-bus. I had the feeling that they'd rather be back in the holding cell at Subic.

The two reluctantly exited the bus with a sort of hang dog look about them.

"You sorry sons of bitches!"

The Gunny went ballistic.

"You two assholes let a SAILOR bring you back?"

With that he hauled off and smacked the Marine closest to him, then turned and cold cocked the second one. They both hit the deck and stayed there.

The Gunny looked at me and took back the arrest reports.

"No offense, sailor," he said.

Believe me, none taken!

* * *

Olongapo City, Luzon, Philippines

The Ensign's New Coffee Mug

Late Summer, 1964

Radarman Second Class Zach Martin needed a smoke. It was 0400 on the morning of September 14, 1964. Martin had been on watch as Supervisor in the Surface Detection Module of the *USS Shangri-La's* CIC — the Combat Information Center — since 2100 of the previous evening. The ship's new operations officer, Commander Klinger, didn't smoke, which meant that no one smoked in CIC...ever!

Martin crossed the passageway and stepped out onto the empty gun sponson across from his Combat Information Center for a quick smoke.

The sponson was nothing more than an empty gun tub with a surrounding guardrail. It was the responsibility of Martin's surface crew to keep the sponson free of rust and salt residue, with a fresh coat of paint to protect it from the harsh lashings of the sea during the not infrequent storms and squalls that the big ship encountered from time to time.

Leaning up against the guardrail, Martin retrieved a pack of Camels from his dungaree shirt pocket, selected a cigarette, and lit it with his ship's emblem *USS Isherwood* Zippo lighter and inhaled deeply. The clear moonlit early morning sky had yet to display the first intrusion from daylight, and a brisk breeze from the ship's sixteen-knot speed embraced his tired body as he tried to let his thoughts drift away from the controlled chaos that usually began long before navigating the eastbound transit of the Strait of Gibraltar.

The ship had recently secured from the Gibraltar Strait navigation detail, which had meant an all hands evolution for CIC as the ship traffic in the narrow strait was one that was fraught with potential collisions; ship traffic moving in to and out from the Mediterranean and numerous small boats crossing back and forth from the African Continent to Europe.

Martin's train of thought was suddenly interrupted by the sound of the sponson's watertight door opening. Phil Luckey, one of Martin's watchstanders, stepped out onto the sponson. Martin nodded and offered him a cigarette from his pack of Camels.

"What's up, man? Want a smoke?"

"Marty, Junior wants to see you in Surface."

"Something up in there that he wants to see me about?"

Luckey shook his head.

"Don't think so, Marty. The radar contact traffic is back to normal. We're down to only four contacts, and they are all opening away."

Martin nodded.

"Tell him that I'll be right in. Don't tell him I'm gonna finish this smoke first."

Luckey smiled and left the sponson headed for CIC.

"Junior" was the nickname for the OI Division Assistant Division Officer, Ensign Scott Gold. Gold was a real piece of work. Barely twenty-three with a bachelor's degree and a few years of NROTC courses at some liberal northeastern college, Ensign Scott Gold, United States Naval Reserve, came aboard knowing everything that needed to be known about the United States Navy in general and aircraft carrier operations in particular — or at least that's what he thought.

Gold was a legend in his own mind who had lost the loyalty of the men assigned to the surface detection module early on when he inappropriately dressed down the division chief, Chief Radarman Roscoe Quarterman in front of the entire OI Division during an in-port training meeting. Chief Quarterman, to his credit, said nothing at the time, waiting for an opportunity to get the young ensign alone for a face-to-face ass-chewing:

"Ensign Gold, lets you and me get somethin' straight right here and now. Number one, you don't ever speak to me like that in front of my men. Number two, you don't know shit about extended forward carrier operations. What you got out of a book in some pissant college don't cut it out here, and you'll be well advised to keep your mouth shut and learn from me and my petty officers just what the hell goes on in this division. You got that?"

"See here, Chief, I…."

"See here my ass, Mister Gold. I been riding carriers for seventeen years, and seven of those years I been an OI division chief. I've washed more salt water out of my goddam socks than you've ever sailed over. I would advise you to watch and learn, and if you've got any criticism, do it privately with me one-on-one."

"We'll see about this insubordinate talk, Chief. I'll be taking this up with Commander Klinger."

"Take it up with the chief of naval operations for all I care, but in the meantime here's another lesson for you to absorb: If you have any complaint about me, you follow chain of command. If you don't you'll get your ass handed to you. If you have a complaint about any of my men that chain starts with me. Don't you ever go over my head."

Martin's thought on how the Navy went about selecting junior officers was interrupted by another sponson visit from Phil Luckey.

"Marty, Mister Gold says to get your ass back in CIC *right now* or you're going on report."

"The 'on report' threat again? Won't be the first time I've heard that. Let's go see what Junior wants this time."

Martin threw the butt of his Camel over the side, left the sponson, and walked into CIC with Luckey. He was pretty sure that he knew what the latest affront to the green officer was about.

"There you are, Martin. Did you have trouble remembering where your watch station was supposed to be?"

Martin gave the young ensign a wide grin, knowing that the grin would further irritate Gold.

"Oh no, sir. Luckey said that you wanted to see me about something, sir?"

"Martin, are you or are you not supposed to be the Surface Watch Supervisor?"

"That I am, sir. Been on watch since midnight and three hours before when we set the navigation detail to transit the Strait."

"Well then if you're the watch supervisor, why aren't you here on watch where you are supposed to be? I came up to check on things only to find you away from your station and out on the sponson doing God knows what all."

"Smoking, sir. Commander Klinger has put the smoking lamp out in CIC."

"I didn't... you... I... see here, Martin, you know damn well what I'm asking, and it isn't a recollection of what you were *doing* out there, but why you weren't where you were *supposed* to be, which is in here supervising the surface watch."

"Oh. I thought you wanted to know what I was doing out there."

Martin saw Luckey standing directly behind Ensign Gold. He was just about doubled up from a Herculean effort to refrain from laughing out loud, which wasn't helping Martin's composure. He struggled to keep a straight face.

"Petty Officer Martin! You are just about to go on report for abandoning your watch station. I want to know why you weren't here on watch when I came in to CIC."

Martin had just about pushed Gold's buttons to the limit. He decided to back off a bit.

"Yes, sir. As I have just said I'd been on watch here since 2100, and Petty Officer Davis, who as you know is a qualified surface watch supervisor, happened to be here. I asked him if he'd mind taking the watch for a bit while I took a break. He said he didn't mind, so I turned over all current information to him and left for a head call and a smoke."

Davis, who was standing nearby, confirmed Martin's comment.

"Yes, sir" Davis agreed. "Martin turned over all of the necessary operating information and turned the watch over to me while he went on a break."

"Davis, when I want your input I'll ask for it. You are supposedly on watch so get back to what you were doing"

It was time for one of the ensign's patented soapbox lectures.

"Martin, the Navy doesn't operate like that. How am I supposed to know who is the supervisor on watch? For that matter how are your watchstanders supposed to know who is in charge?"

"Well, Mister Gold," Martin answered, "you could have asked someone on watch. They would have told you that Davis had relieved me.

If Ensign Gold had been a balloon, everyone in CIC would have been able to hear the air being let out of the nozzle.

"Well, it certainly seems to me that someone could have notified me when I came in."

Martin couldn't help himself. He knew that all this business about the watch was just the preamble to Gold's real reason for gunning for him.

"Watch change. Yes, sir. From now on if you'd be good enough to ask someone we'll avoid all this unpleasantness."

Gold could barely maintain his composure.

"Martin, before you resume the watch I want you to put your insubordinate cracks on hold and walk into the Countermeasures Module with me. There is something that needs explaining in there."

The Countermeasures Module was a small space located directly opposite the Surface Module where two of Martin's specially trained watchstanders manned receiver consoles that continually searched the Soviet and Soviet Bloc military frequencies looking for any radar signatures from the Soviet naval and air forces that may be operating in the area whose missile or aircraft acquisition radars might present a threat to the ship.

All that is very well and good, but on this early morning Ensign Scott Gold, United States Naval Reserve, was not interested in Soviet Bloc radars. Ensign Gold was about to interrogate Martin with questions regarding the CIC coffee mess, which was in the Countermeasures Module. More specifically, Ensign Gold wished to know the whereabouts of his shiny new, annotated with name and rank…coffee mug!

"Martin…where is my coffee mug?"

"Pardon, Mister Gold?"

"Martin, goddamit, you know exactly what I'm talking about. Before we left Mayport I had purchased a coffee mug that had my name above a gold ensign's bar and my rank beneath it. On the opposite side was the insignia of a naval officer. That mug cost me seventeen dollars, and as I look at the mug board I see that my mug is not on its assigned hook."

"Seventeen dollars seems a bit high, Mister Gold. Where the hell did you buy it?"

"Martin…I…you…the cost of the mug is irrelevant. Do you see that the damn mug is not where it is supposed to be?"

Martin was amazed at how quickly the veins on the side of the ensign's neck could pop up.

"Might be irrelevant to you, Mister Gold, but it damn sure wouldn't be to me. To answer your question, yes, I do see that the mug is not there.

"Is that all, sir? I'd like to get back on watch."

"No, Martin that is *not* all. When we left the States I specifically placed you in charge of ensuring that nothing happened to my mug and that it remained clean and on the mug board, ready for use when I came on watch. Do you remember that?"

"Yes, Mister Gold, I remember the conversation."

"It wasn't a conversation, sailor. It was a direct order."

Martin quickly reviewed his options. He decided on his original plan, to confront Ensign Gold about the order to maintain Gold's coffee mug

"Mister Gold, after we left Mayport and you ordered me as senior watch supervisor to be responsible for your seventeen-dollar mug I reviewed the ship's CIC Doctrine book and couldn't find any mention of the senior watch supervisor being responsible for the assistant division officer's coffee mug. I then assumed that because you were new you took what should have been a request and misspoke when you gave a direct order."

Ensign Gold was fast approaching a state of apoplexy.

"Martin, where is my coffee mug?"

Martin shrugged.

"Mister Gold, I haven't the slightest idea. Maybe you left it in the wardroom. Why don't you ask one of the stewards?"

"Petty Officer Martin, you had damn well better watch your step. Before I'm done I'll be sure that you are busted down to seaman."

"Yes, sir. I'm sure you will try your best. And if you do manage to do it, it certainly won't be because I didn't babysit your seventeen-dollar coffee mug."

"Get back and resume your watch before I write you up."

"Yes, sir."

*   *   *

Martin hadn't been in his rack very long when Yeoman Third Class Orville Barton descended the ladder steps into the darkened OI Division berthing compartment. Barton, the division office clerk, came over to Martin's aisle and focused the beam of his flashlight on the middle bunk.

"Marty wake up! Marty get up! Mister Gray wants to see you in the Division Office right away."

"Shit! What time is it, Barton?"

"0945. And Mister Gray wants to see you most scratchie."

"Damn! I only hit the rack two hours ago. Let me put some water on my face, and I'll be right up."

Martin heaved himself clumsily out of his canvas rack and walked slowly into the head. What he really needed was a cigarette, but Klinger had put the smoking lamp out in the OI office and compartment as well. Martin didn't want to keep the CIC Officer, Lieutenant Commander Gray waiting. He liked Mister Gray. He was a straight shooter and a good officer.

The young petty officer bent over the steel sink, hurriedly splashed some water on his face and returned to his bunk where his dungaree working uniform from the day before was hanging on a bunk chain. He put on the shirt and trousers, laced up his black, steel-toed chukka boots and went up the ladder steps toward the OI Division office, which was in an admin space just forward from CIC.

Martin arrived at the office within ten minutes of the wakeup call from Barton. He walked through the door and found Lieutenant Commander Gray, Ensign Gold, and Chief Quarterman waiting for him. Gray was the first to speak.

"Sorry we had to get you out of your rack, Martin. I know that you haven't had much sleep lately, but we've received notification from NavAirLant that help is on the way. We will have a first-class petty officer waiting for us when we arrive at Cannes. I'm going to put him over on the Surface side, as the Air side is manned up well, and Surface is shorthanded. He'll be taking the leading petty officer duties from you, but I plan to put him on the at sea watchstander bill to give you and Davis a breather."

'I know he didn't wake me up to tell me that I wasn't getting enough sleep. Gold's over there looking like he's about to bust.'

"Thank you, Mister Gray. Davis and I can use some help in Surface."

Gray turned and addressed Ensign Gold,

"Scott, I think we've finished going over the division manning problems. The men have been on short sleep for almost two weeks, and everyone is a bit short fused. Why don't you let Chief Quarterman and I have a consultation with Martin here? I'll call you if we need anything more from you in this area."

"John, I just want…"

"Fine, Scott. The Chief and I will take it from here."

Gold was clearly disappointed that he wouldn't be present for what he thought would be Martin's going on report.

Once the ensign had cleared the office Chief Quarterman turned to Martin and spoke,

"Marty, just what the hell went on this morning on watch?"

"Chief, I'd been on watch since 2100 the night before when we set the navigation detail to transit the Strait and had to assume surface supervisor when the detail secured. At around 0330 or so Davis came in and relieved me so I could take a head break and catch a smoke on the sponson. Right after that, Gold...er Mister Gold came in and wanted to know where I was. When Luckey came out to tell me that Mister Gold wanted me in CIC I finished my smoke and went back inside."

Lieutenant Commander Gray addressed a question to Martin,

"And that was it, Martin? That's why he's so upset?"

"Well..., no, sir."

Chief Quarterman had a follow up question.

"Ensign Gold says that you were not only insubordinate, but that you did something with his coffee mug. What the hell is that all about?"

Martin shrugged his shoulders.

"When we left Mayport for the Mediterranean, Mister Gold gave me a direct order that I was to be responsible for his coffee mug, which I was supposed to have clean and ready for use whenever he walked in to CIC."

"WHAT? HE DID WHAT?"

Gray looked like he didn't hear what was just said.

Martin began to think that he might get out of this after all.

"Yes, sir. Said it was a direct order, and when he came in to CIC last night and went to the mug board, his mug wasn't there. He accused me of losing it."

Quarterman was about to speak when Gray motioned for him to be silent.

"And what was your response to that, Martin?"

Martin paused a bit before responding. Then he thought, '*What the hell might as well let it fly.*'

"Well, sir, I told him that I had reviewed the CIC Doctrine folder and that I couldn't find anything in it that said the senior watch supervisor had to baby sit his mug. I said I didn't know where his mug was and that maybe he should ask the wardroom stewards where the thing was."

For a minute the young petty officer thought he saw a momentary flash of anger cross Gray's face, but he couldn't be sure whether Gray's anger was directed toward him ensign...or both.

That point was soon cleared up. It seemed like one hell of a long time before Gray spoke,

"Martin, you may have noticed that Ensign Gold can be a bit...shall we say...overenthusiastic upon occasion. It is to everyone's benefit that we have patience with him and try to gently guide him along the path to becoming a useful and pro-ductive officer. Mister Gold came in this morning wanting to place you on report and send you to Captain's Mast, and from the way he described the encounter, he may be well within the boundaries of naval regulations to do so."

"Yes, sir."

"I personally do not think that anyone benefits from that. The Captain, as you may imagine, is a very busy man and would probably tell Commander Klinger to handle his own laundry. I'll tell you here and now that the last thing that any-one wants to do in this division is ruffle Commander Klinger's feathers..."

'Shit rolls downhill.'

"...so, here's what we're going to do. From right now going forward I want you to stop *fucking* with Ensign Gold, because if he comes to me one more time with allegations of your wise-ass-ing to him I'll have your stripes and have you transferred out of here to some Godforsaken amphib or auxiliary ship so fast that your head will spin. Is ...that... clear?"

"Abundantly so, Mister Gray."

"Good. I will, in turn, counsel Mister Gold as to just what to expect of his supervisors on watch and which sort of orders are appropriate and which are not. To be clear, Mister Gold can-not order someone to... as you so colorfully stated...baby sit his coffee mug. He was mistaken in that, but you are also culpable in your response to his error.

"Is that also clear?"

"Absolutely, sir."

"Good. Now, Chief, if you and Martin will go about whatever else you have planned, I have work to do before flight quarters this afternoon."

Chief Quarterman and Martin responded in unison with a crisp, "Yes, sir," got up, and left the office. Martin couldn't get out of there fast enough!

Once they were outside the office and in the passageway Chief Quarterman turned to Martin and asked,

"Alright Marty, what did you do with Junior's precious cup?"

"You mean his beautiful mug? I threw the fucking thing over the side the second day after we left port."

*   *   *

USS Shangri-La (CVA 38)

Patsy and the Tyke

Summer, 1965

Martin and the "Tyke" exited the water taxi at the fleet landing pier on Harbor Drive. *Hissem*, *Calcaterra*, *Stroud* and *Vance*
had entered San Diego Bay on the June 5th morning tide and
secured themselves to two of the harbor mooring buoys designated for Navy use. *Hissem* and *Calcaterra* were nested to mooring buoy 26, while *Stroud* and *Vance* were nested together at
buoy 27 downstream.

"Tyke, do you plan to head out somewhere or would
you care to run with me seeing as I've been homeported here
before?"

The Tyke smiled.

"I got no damned camera around my neck and I'm not
interested in taking a tour. When a sailor goes ashore after a
period at sea he wants to accomplish three things: get drunk, get
laid and get in a fight. If he manages to do two of the three it's
considered a good liberty. If you don't mind, I'll hang with you
today and we can see what the town has to offer."

Martin nodded and pointed toward Broadway, the main
avenue leading to downtown San Diego.

"Let's head up Broadway and wet our whistle at the Seven
Seas Bar and Locker Club up the street. Then we can head to a
few places where they may remember me."

"Lead the way, Marty. Nuthin' I love more than hittin' the
beach in a new liberty port."

*   *   *

The Seven Seas Bar and Locker Club, located on Broadway
several blocks to the east of fleet landing was more than just
a bar. Seven Seas was a tailor shop, a clothier, a place where a
sailor could come ashore in uniform, go to a rented locker in
the large locker room on the second floor, unlock the locker
door padlock which he had purchased at Seven Seas, remove
his non regulation gabardine uniform which he may have purchased and had tailored at Seven Seas, don a pair of civilian

pants and sports shirt which he may have purchased at Seven Seas, and head for the bar where if he was of age could buy a drink. In short, the folks at Seven Seas made sure that no matter what a sailor wanted or needed – excluding women - Seven Seas had it, including ship's patches, hash marks, rating badges, even Zippo lighters with engraved ship's name and silhouette could be purchased.

Martin and the Tyke were not interested in purchasing anything other than a cold beer or two, a commodity in great supply at the bar which ran the entire length of the building's right wall.

"How 'bout a cold one, Tyke? I'm buying the first round."

"Great! I've got a sponsor. Don't suppose they have any 'Gansetts out here, do they?"

"Can't say as they do, but I've got a pretty good replacement in mind if you're game."

"Hell Marty, you're buying. Go for it."

The bartender walked over to the two sailors, looked them over and decided that they were both of age.

"What'll it be gents?"

Martin addressed the barkeep's question.

"Two Oles please, my friend."

The bartender nodded.

"Coming right up. Draft or bottle?"

"Draft is good."

The bartender paused for a moment and looked at Martin closely.

"You look kinda familiar, sailor. Are you homeported here?"

Martin shook his head.

"Used to be homeported here on the *Isherwood*. I'd stop in now and then when Linda was working. She still work here?"

The bartender shook his head.

"Nope. She quit about six months ago. Married a sailor from some minesweeper up in Long Beach."

Martin was disappointed.

"Too bad. She had a nice set of cans."

The bartender nodded.

"Talk of the town. Now let me get those drafts for you. My name is Shakey."

The Tyke smiled. "Shakey, how'd you ever get hooked with that name?"

The bartender smiled. "Spent eleven years in the Navy doing explosive ordnance disposal."

The three men laughed.

"Nah, I just tell the customers that. I got the name because I mix the best vodka martini in town. Let me get you boys those beers."

Shakey retrieved two chilled12 ounce glasses from the cooler behind the bar, walked over to the beer taps, deftly poured two glasses of Olympia drafts and returned.

"Here you go, gents. That'll be seventy cents."

Martin placed a five-dollar bill on the bar.

"Here you go, Shakey. Name's Marty and this is my ship-mate Tyke. Have one yourself."

"Thanks for the offer Marty. I don't drink while I'm work-ing. I like it too much. If it's alright with you I'll take out for one when I go off shift."

"Absolutely. Help yourself."

Shakey extended his hand. Martin took it and the two men shook hands. He then walked to the register, rang up the drinks and returned with Martin's change.

"Good health, men. Welcome to San Diego and the Seven Seas. What ship? You guys going to be here for a while?"

The Tyke answered Eli's questions, offering as little infor-mation regarding the ship's movement as possible.

"We're on the *Stroud* headed with three other cans to Pearl. Change of home port from Newport. We'll be here for a few days to take on fuel and stores and then we're on our way."

Shakey nodded.

"Well Tyke if you're paired up with a guy who knew Linda you're in for a great port visit. Enjoy your stay."

The bartender turned and walked down the bar to attend to some sailors who had just arrived.

Tyke turned to Martin and smiled.

"What's the story with Linda, Marty? Did the two of you hook up?"

Martin thought for a moment before answering.

"Linda was in her mid to late thirties when I knew her which would make her a bit over forty now. She was a pure looker. You knew she was getting up there but man! Was she ever put together!"

The Tyke nodded as Martin continued.

"Linda was no Rhodes Scholar, but she was bright, sincere and if she had a sailor friend in trouble she'd do all she could to help him.

Martin continued with the story of his first meeting with Linda.

"The cops here in San Diego don't much care for sailors, I guess because they have to deal with so many of these young kids who get drunk and cause problems. Look at a patrol car the next time one drives by. You'll see that the cops wear helmets even when they are in the car. Right off the bat you know they'll be prone to knocking heads first and asking questions later. If you get busted here, you get a much better reception from the Shore Patrol rather than the city cops.

"The first time I was here I didn't know much about San Diego. I was on the *McKean* back then. Couldn't have been more than nineteen. The ship was down here from Long Beach for six weeks of refresher training and I decided I was going to check out Tijuana with a couple of guys from Navigation Division who had been here before.

"Well, we got off the water taxi and headed up here to Seven Seas to rent some civvies as you couldn't cross the border in uniform.

"I rented a shirt and pair of slacks for the one day, I think it cost me a dollar, and we jumped on the bus for San Ysidro and crossed the border to T-town."

Tyke was listening intently as Martin's story unfolded.

"I had never seen anything like it before. We walked into a joint by the name of Tio Pepe's just across from a jai alai fronton. A waiter came up and Mullarkey - he was a quartermaster on the ship - told the waiter to bring us a round of Tecates. He then pointed to me and told the waiter that this was my first time in T-Town and to give me a shot of tequila with the Tecate.

"The next thing I knew there was this cute little honey sitting next to me. She put her hand on my thigh right next to my johnson and started rubbing. Kind of spooked me because it happened so quickly. I must have really looked surprised, Mullarkey was laughing his ass off.

"I threw back the tequila shot and chased it with a drink from the Tecate. Damn stuff tasted like liquid fire. All the while this bar girl was rubbing my johnson faster and faster. I was beginning not to mind so much."

The Tyke smiled.

"I can see where this is going."

"Yep. And it got there after two more tequilas and two bar drinks for the girl. She invited me upstairs for a little 'short time.' The third tequila and her "thigh" massage had by this time worn down any objections I might have had, and we went upstairs to a little alcove with a cot, wash basin and water pitcher where she put me through the wringer in about three minutes flat."

"Three minutes?"

"Yep. Three minutes. She was a real pro.

"When we left T-town I was kind of 'over served' you might say and by the time I got back to Seven Seas my two shipmates had left me to fend for myself."

Tyke shook his head.

"Marty, they aren't much good for shipmates if they left you like that."

Martin nodded his assent and continued.

"I was having a lot of trouble walking but I did manage to change back to my uniform and was leaving the Seven Seas when a woman who I later got to know was the night bartender took me by the arm and said she'd get me back to Fleet Landing safely once she got off shift so the cops wouldn't pick me up."

"And this was Linda?"

"Yep. She must have taken pity on me, a baby-faced kid who was knee skinnin', commode huggin' drunk. Anyway, she guided me around the corner to her car and drove me back to Fleet Landing where I boarded the water taxi and puked my guts out on the way back to the ship."

The Tyke had a question.

"Why didn't you ask to go home with her?"

Martin laughed.

"Man, I didn't know which one to ask. I was seeing three of her - and everything else for that matter."

The Tyke laughed.

"The evils of strong drink strike again, shipmate."

Martin nodded.

"Yep. At any rate I'm glad I didn't. Three days later I came down with a roaring dose of the clap...and crabs! Went to Captain's mast about it and was given thirty days restriction to the ship. I didn't run into Linda again until I came back here for duty on the *Isherwood.*

"Tyke, unless you want to hang around here there are a couple of more places I'd like to hit today. Seven Seas has always been more of a 'coming and going' stop for me. You know, one to start the day and one for a nightcap."

The Tyke wanted to see more of the San Diego gut. He was in total agreement.

"Works for me. It's time for you to show your leading petty officer another of the San Diego sailor bars."

Both men left a dollar tip for Shakey, exited the Seven Seas and headed east on Broadway for several blocks then turned south for the two-block walk to F Street. Turning east again they walked a short distance to the Broadway Theater, an aging burlesque theater which was located next to the Sportsman's Palace. The Sportsman's Palace was to be the next stop for the two sailors.

The Sportsman's Palace was owned by a retired Vaudeville song and dance man named Bob Morgan who also owned the Broadway Burlesque Theater next door. Both establishments were anachronisms, a throwback to the hustle and bustle of the forties and earlier. During World War II the influx of sailors and Marines who were stationed in San Diego and in nearby towns filled the theater and the bar next door to capacity every afternoon, evening and night which made Morgan a multi-millionaire and allowed him to purchase a stable of thoroughbred race horses. Morgan also had dabbled in the 'sweet science' as a youth and had a reputation for being a reasonably decent lightweight boxer in his day.

The décor of the bar left no doubt to the casual observer as to Morgan's passions. The walls and the back bar were filled with framed photographs of racing horses, boxers and vaudeville stars of years past. On most afternoons Morgan could be found sitting at the table near the entrance drinking coffee. It was not uncommon for the performers past and present from the theater next door and the occasional old boxer to join Morgan and his choreographer wife Franny at their table for a few drinks and a lot of reminiscence.

Martin and the Tyke entered the saloon and occupied two stools at the bar. The bartender, a tall, tattooed middle aged man walked down the bar to serve them.

"Damn! You leave the door unlocked and you never know who'll walk in. Marty, how the hell are you? Long time no see."

"Smitty, it's good to be back, at least for a while. We're on our way to Pearl so I told the Captain that we might as well stop in San Diego while we're on the way. This is my shipmate Charlie Zeimet. Everyone calls him Tyke.

"Tyke, this is my favorite bartender, Smitty. Smitty is a retired first-class Navy weather guesser who was so bad at predicting the weather all he can do now is tend bar."

Smitty shook his head and smiled.

"Some people never change, even junior petty officers like you, Marty. Anyway, welcome back. Tyke glad to meet you although you could choose better company to run with.

"You guys here for long?"

Tyke shook Smitty's extended hand and replied.

"Just long enough to refuel and resupply then we're off to Pearl Harbor for a home port change from Newport. As for being seen in public with Marty, he's the only one in the division who's been here before. Got no choice."

Smitty smiled.

"Well I guess we'll cut you some slack. What'll it be today, guys?"

"I'll have a Bacardi and Coke, Smitty. What about you, Tyke."

"Sounds good. Make it two, Smitty."

"Comin' right up."

Smitty walked over to the back bar and retrieved a bottle of Bacardi light rum and began to pour the drink order.

"Hi sailor. Come here often?"

The husky, sultry voice of Patsy Coolidge whispered in Martin's ear.

Martin turned slightly to his right to see an attractive mid-thirties redhead in a low-cut cocktail dress.

"Patsy! I'd know your sexy voice anywhere. How are you honey? On a break from next door?"

"Nope. I'm not next door for the next six weeks. Got a gig at the airport. Chamber of Commerce hired a trio to greet the incoming passengers and the trio hired me to sing a few tunes with them on weekends. Easy work, good pay. Just the way I like it."

Martin gestured toward Tyke.

"Patsy, this is my shipmate Charlie Zeimet, better known as the Tyke."

Tyke grinned and extended his hand.

"Hi Patsy. Marty didn't tell me he knew such a good-looking woman here in San Diego. I am *very* pleased to meet you."

Patsy Coolidge shook Tyke's hand and put on her vamp smile. If she had been a cat you could have heard her purr clear across the room.

"Ooh, Marty, he's cute. Says the right things too. Can I keep him for a while?"

"Patsy, the lad is one-and twenty. And then some. There is no extra charge if you want to sweep him off his feet while we're in town."

Patsy took a seat at the bar next to the Tyke, ordered a gin and tonic and addressed her new-found friend.

"Tyke, I've just finished the gig at the airport for today and I'm on the way home to change. I should be about a half hour to forty-five minutes tops. Mind waiting for me? There are a few local haunts I'd like to visit and if you're not joined at the hip with Marty I'd like for you to join me."

Tyke turned to Marty and with a wide grin on his face spoke in a low voice:

"I owe you *big time* for this, buddy.

"Tell me tomorrow morning and I'll believe you. You better have plenty of cash."

Tyke smiled and patted his pocket.

"Not a problem, shipmate. Got a wallet full."

Tyke summoned the bartender with a quick hand gesture.

"Smitty, take the money for the young lady's drink here. And if she'd care for another it's on my tab."

Patsy Coolidge smiled and drained the gin and tonic that Smitty had set in front of her."

"Once again please, Smitty. The gentleman wants to buy me another."

Martin smiled to himself.

'*A match made in heaven,*' he thought. "*I can't wait to hear the Tyke's story tomorrow aboard ship.*'

Smitty served the second gin and tonic to Patsy who offered her glass in a toast.

"Thanks for the refreshment, Tyke. May you be in heaven thirty minutes before the devil knows you're dead."

Tyke touched Patsy's glass with his own and replied in his best faux Irish brogue.

"A lovely toast from a lovely lass, I'm sure."

Smitty was trying his best to stifle a smile, and in his ever-helpful role as bartender and matchmaker offered a suggestion.

"Patsy, why waste time and gas going home to change and then having to come back here to pick up Tyke? Take him with you and he can wait while you change, then you can show him some San Diego night life."

Patsy turned to the Tyke and smiled her vamp smile again for him.

"You don't mind, do you honey? I won't be long. You'll have to excuse the mess in my apartment. I hadn't planned on company."

The Tyke was grinning from ear to ear.

"Not a bit. Let's have one more round on me before we go."

The third round arrived swiftly and was equally as swiftly dispatched.

"Ready, honey? I'm parked just down the block."

"Ready and willing, Patsy. Marty, I'll see you back on-board ship."

Martin smiled and gave the Tyke a thumbs-up. The Tyke and Patsy nodded at Smitty and hurriedly left the bar.

Once the two were out of earshot Marty turned to Smitty and offered a prediction.

"Smitty, that's what I call helping out a shipmate. If the Tyke is gonna get laid it'll have to be as soon as they get to the apartment. If I know Patsy at all I know she'll be shit faced before the sun sets, and after that she'll be causing trouble wherever they go."

"Well Marty, you know you could have told him not to go with her. I didn't see you coming to his rescue."

"Nope. Tyke has a woody that's left him with not enough skin to blink his eyes. Can't talk to a guy when he is thinking with the little head. I figure the Tyke thinks he scooped me by swooping Patsy out of here."

"Marty, are you and the Tyke in the same division aboard ship?"

Martin smiled. "He's my division lead petty officer."

Smitty rolled his eyes and offered a further thought on how the Tyke and Patsy's day together would unfold.

"Here's my prediction, Marty. By 2100 Patsy will have her nasty drunk on and will have some drunk sailor or barfly making a run on her. The situation will escalate until she turns to your buddy and says something like 'Are you gonna let him talk to me like that?' Then it'll be fist city until the shore patrol or the cops or both arrive, your buddy gets caught up in the net and winds up at shore patrol headquarters with a brand-new set of bumps and bruises.

"And I'll give you five to one odds on that all-day long."

Zack Martin grinned.

"No bet, Smitty."

*   *   *

The cab dropped Martin off at fleet landing the next morning just in time to catch the water taxi back to the *Stroud*.

"Marty!"

Martin looked up in the general direction of the water taxi's bow.

"Tyke! Jesus, what happened to you? You look like you've been ridden hard and put away wet."

Charlie "The Tyke" Zeimet was sitting forward near the water taxi bow. He had no hat, no neckerchief and a torn jumper. His right eye was slightly swollen, and his right cheek was bruised. There was dried blood on his upper lip beneath his nose.

"What happened to me? Is that your question? Your goddam friend Patsy is a nut job, that's what happened to me."

Martin nodded his agreement.

"Yeah, you're right there. Exactly what the hell happened?"

Zeimet waved a typewritten document which he pulled from his breast pocket.

"Well, you can read about it in this shore patrol incident report if you like."

A smiling Zack Martin declined the offer.

"No, no. My guess is your version is more interesting. Start with when you left me at the saloon."

Zeimet heaved a long sigh.

"We got to her apartment and she was right...the place looked like a rat's nest. She went into the bedroom while I cleared a place and sat on the couch to wait for her. I hadn't been sitting for two minutes when she came out of the bedroom *butt naked!*"

"Ah, the plot thickens. Continue."

"Yeah. Well, I got the none too subtle message and headed for the bedroom with her. We stayed there all afternoon. She was *fantastic* in bed.

"Later that evening Patsy said, 'Let's go out and get something to eat.' We got dressed and headed out to some chain coffee shop on the main drag and grabbed a sandwich."

Martin nodded.

"So far, so good Tyke. What I want to know is how you got busted up?"

Zeimet affected a disgusted look and continued the narrative.

"Yeah, me too. Happened kinda quick, ya know?

"Patsy had me in tow for most of the evening. We must have hit about half a dozen joints and she was knockin' back the gin and tonics like they were gonna go out of style the next day."

Martin gave the Tyke a nod. He had heard about Patsy's antics when she had a gin drunk going for her.

"Shipmate, I can see where this is headed. Patsy got her gin drunk on, right?"

Zeimet nodded, then shook his head in disbelief. A look of disgust crossed his bruised face.

"Nasty as a fuckin' rattlesnake. Every joint we hit she'd knock back a few of them damn gin and tonics and start an argument with someone at the bar."

Zeimet continued with his narrative of the preceding night.

"We were eighty-sixed out of the last bar before we walked into this skid row joint about three blocks down from the

Sportsman's Palace and took a seat at the bar. Patsy sat next to this big Godzilla lookin' son-of-a-bitch who was about as drunk as Patsy.

"Well, it looked to me like they knew each other because she started in on him right away, said he wasn't a real man and shit like that.

"The big guy didn't say anything at first, but you could tell he was steamed by just looking at him.

"Patsy ordered a double gin. I was beginning to think that as good as that pussy was maybe it wasn't *that* good as I could see trouble brewing. I suggested we call it a night and that I had to get back to the ship.

"It was like she never heard me. I told the bartender to close me out and he walked down to the end of the bar to make change from my twenty. Then I heard Patsy announce to everyone at the bar that this big guy couldn't even...how'd she say it?... oh yeah, said he couldn't get it up and he wasn't a *real* man like... me!

"Just about that time Godzilla turned and looked directly at me. He had murder in his eye and started to get up from his stool when Patsy threw her drink in his face!

"Godzilla wasn't too happy about Patsy wetting him down and he threw a punch at her. Patsy ducked, and I got hit square below the eye."

Martin began to laugh.

"It's not fuckin' funny, Marty."

"Sorry Tyke. I was just seeing all that in my mind."

"And that was it? End of story?"

Tyke shook his head.

"Oh no. I wish it was. Patsy picked up Godzilla's beer bottle and laid it upside his head, which only seemed to piss him off more.

"He grabbed my neckerchief and got ready to take a swing at me. I ducked down and my neckerchief slipped over my grease collar and head. The guy's punch landed on my right eye but not as hard as it would have if I was still attached to my neckerchief. Just kind of grazed me.

"Meanwhile drunk Patsy climbed up on his back and is giving him those girly swats and working him over with her nails.

"Godzilla grabbed me in a bear hug. Patsy was still up on his back. The three of us fell on the floor and all you could see was assholes and elbows. He's swinging at me, I'm tucked up to the guy as close as I could get...by the way he smelled like he hadn't had a bath in a week... anyhow I'm as close as I could get so his punches won't fuckin' kill me, Patsy's on top of him kickin' and screamin' at the top of her lungs when...."

"Hahahahahaha, I'm sorry Tyke, can't help it. The picture of all that is just too funny."

Charlie "The Tyke" Zeimet was not amused. He gave Martin a sobering stare and continued with his story.

"... the cops arrived with a shore patrolman with them."

"So, you took a ride to the San Diego lockup?"

Zeimet shook his head.

"Nope. One cop pulled Patsy off Godzilla and she began slapping the cop. Big mistake. The cop coldcocked her with one punch and handcuffed her while the other cop and the shore patrol tried to separate Godzilla and me, the cop was whacking Godzilla with his night stick and the shore patrol sailor was pulling me by my jumper, which caused it to rip.

"Between the two of them they got us apart and the cops called for another squad car because they didn't want the big guy and Patsy in the same car. The shore patrol called for the patrol van to haul me off to patrol headquarters."

Martin was stunned.

"Sorry, Tyke. I knew Patsy was a handful, but I sure didn't think you'd wind up at shore patrol headquarters."

Zeimet shrugged.

"Shit happens, not to worry. They didn't get my maidenhead when they hauled me in. Anyway, I touched all three bases on my liberty list. Got drunk, got laid, got in a fight. Now I just have to sweat what the XO and the Captain will do about this."

~To be continued~

*   *   *

7 Seas Locker Club & Clothiers Ad circa 1965

The Tyke Visits the XO

Summer, 1965

Zack Martin gestured toward the *Stroud* as the water taxi made its approach to the quarterdeck ladder.

"Looks like you'll have the answer to that right away. Our division officer has the OOD watch and XO's standing there right beside him."

"Shit! Looks like the incident report beat me here."

The two sailors exited the taxi and boarded the *Stroud*. The ship's XO, Lieutenant Pierce motioned Martin and Zeimet to come over to where he was standing.

"Martin, I don't see your name on this incident report. How'd you manage that?"

Zeimet began to offer clarification.

"XO, Martin and I....."

"Shut up Tyke. I'm talking to Martin. What about it Martin? Were you with Zeimet when all this went down?"

Martin shook his head, indicating that the two sailors were not together.

"No sir. We were together earlier but we got separated in the afternoon."

XO had a puzzled look on his face.

"But you both came back together this morning. How'd that happen?"

Martin clarified.

"It was the luck of the draw, sir. I boarded the water taxi and Zeimet was already aboard."

"So then, you have nothing to add that would explain how your leading petty officer returned in a torn and dirty uniform after spending the night as a guest of the shore patrol?"

Martin shook his head.

Well, no sir not really."

"Not really? What the hell does that mean? Did you, or didn't you?"

"Well sir we split up around 1400 yesterday afternoon after I introduced Zeimet to a girl that I knew from when I was home ported here a few years ago."

The XO rubbed his hand across his brow.

"Christ. Don't tell me I'm going to have two of you to deal with going forward. Alright Zeimet, you and Martin go get ready for morning quarters. Zeimet report to my stateroom immediately following quarters for muster."

"Aye, sir."

The two men saluted Lieutenant Pierce and headed forward toward the division berthing compartment, changed into their dungaree working uniforms and proceeded to the port side of the 01-deck level for muster with the division officer, Lieutenant (junior grade) Dooley.

*   *   *

Quarters for muster had finished and the men headed for their work assignments for the day. Mister Dooley motioned for Zeimet to remain.

"Zeimet, I believe you have an appointment with the XO and I'd like to see you immediately after."

Zeimet nodded his assent.

"Yes sir."

"Right. Get going to your appointment and report back to me when you're finished."

Zeimet saluted and left the formation. Arriving at the XO's stateroom shortly thereafter he knocked on the stateroom door.

"Enter."

Zeimet opened the stateroom door and entered the room. XO was at his desk.

"Tyke, before I take care of this incident report I have just one question."

"Yes, sir XO. What is it?"

"Are you blackmailing the Captain?"

"I'm sorry XO. What was that again?"

"A simple enough question, Tyke. Are you blackmailing the Captain, yes or no?"

"No sir. Why would you ask?"

"Last night I got a call from the Captain at around 2200. He wanted to take a walkthrough of the ship to check readiness for getting underway. We happened to be on the quarterdeck talking with Chief Harper who happened to be OOD when the water taxi came alongside, and a shore patrolman came aboard with your incident report. He handed the report to Chief Harper and said they'd be releasing you in the morning."

"The Captain took the report and read it. Then he shook his head and laughed. He told me to handle this on an informal level, so your service record could remain clean."

"Yes sir."

"So Zeimet, what is your side of the story?"

Zeimet began stating his defense.

"Believe me XO, I'm collateral damage here. I met this girl at a local watering hole and we kind of hung out for the day and hit a few bars. I didn't know at the time she was a lush and a nasty drunk and when she threw her drink into this big son-of-a-bitch's face he came after me."

"After that I was just hanging on so the guy wouldn't kill me. Then Patsy – she's the girl - climbs on his back and starts swearing and slapping him. Shortly after that the cops showed up and... well, you know the rest."

LT Pierce pushed back in his swivel chair and spoke.

"Zeimet I'm sure you're aware that there are some young sailors in your division that see you coming back from liberty bruised and wearing a torn and dirty uniform and think they should emulate that kind of behavior, the kind of behavior that could get them in trouble or possibly in danger of being injured, is that what you want?"

"No sir XO. I see your point."

"Exactly. Here's what I propose to drive home the point. It will be a while before you get to examine any Hawaiian palm trees up close and personal. I'm proposing that you restrict yourself to the ship while she is in port for a period of twenty-one in-port days. Of course, if you feel the need to pursue this issue at mast we can do so. You realize that there's no telling whether the Captain will be in a good mood on that day. In fact, your presence at mast after he wished to dispose of this matter informally may very well piss him off to the point where the possibility of losing a stripe cannot be ruled out."

"XO, you know me. I'm not the kind of guy to make waves. Restriction is fine."

"Then it's settled. Twenty-one in port days beginning when we get to Pearl."

"Yes sir."

"Good. That's all then, Tyke. I expect you have a lot to do to prepare CIC for sea on the 8th as do I. Off you go."

"Aye sir. Thank you."

"Tyke, one more thing."

"Yes, sir XO, what is it?"

"In the future choose your whores with a bit more discretion."

"Your mouth to God's ears, XO."

XO displayed a hint of a smile on his face.

"I said off you go, Tyke. Out, before I change my mind."

*　*　*

Destroyer Escort Stroud

"Dumber Than a Bag of Hammers"

The three-month shipyard period passed quickly for me – I was having a rather intense affair with an eighteen-year old married woman who decided to break it off when our ship got underway for a refresher training period in San Diego, and I had been transferred to the operations department where I was to strike – that is work and study - in the Radarman career path in the Combat Information Center without the benefit of attending the multi-week Radarman "A" training school back at the Great Lakes Naval Training Center. There were only three of us in OI Division who hadn't been through the formal training there; Jerry Beatty, Bobby Joe Solomon and me. Beatty was due to leave the Navy within a few months, and Solomon…well…

*   *   *

Spring, 1959
I was taking a quick smoke break on the fantail, enjoying the balmy Hawaiian breezes when my former lead seaman from 2nd Division, Granny Miller joined me.

"Hey man, what's up with all that spooky looking shit they puttin' in your space on the 01-deck? Nobody know what the fuck goin' down. Where we goin' anyway?"

The day after we arrived at Pearl Harbor the ship was invaded by a host of civilian technicians and several men in jump-suits with "NASA" patches sewn on the left breast pocket area. To further heighten the crew's curiosity several Air Force officers had arrived and were busily consulting with the NASA people.

I gave Granny the "amphibious salute," a shrug of the shoulders.

"Beats me, Granny. I'm paddling around in the smallest canoe in the lake up there. The ops officer and division officer know but they aren't talking. Word has it that the Captain has told the wardroom to keep their mouths shut about whatever is going on."

"Mmmm Mm. Must be some heavy shit goin' on with all them spooks and flyboys runnin' around up there, in and out of your space all day.

Let me know if you hear anything, okay, man?"

"No problem, Granny. Soon as I hear anything I'll cut you in."

I flipped the butt of my Camel cigarette over the side and headed forward to the ladder that would take me to the 01-deck and CIC. I scaled the ladder and opened the door to the Combat Information Center. My watch section supervisor, Radarman Third Charlie Floyd was perched on a stool by our dead-reckon navigation table, or DRT, using the glass table top to make pen and ink corrections to a few of the operations publications that we used daily when underway. Most of the publications were "Allied friendly," meaning that when we were operating with ships of a foreign navy that were considered an ally we'd be able to speak the same language when executing a joint allied tactical maneuver or using specific alpha-numeric "signal" words when communicating.

"Anything going on back on the fantail?"

I shook my head. "Nope. Just ship's work and Granny Miller quizzing me on what all the activity in our storeroom is about.

"Have you heard anything, Charlie?"

Floyd gave me his "cat that ate the canary" grin.

"Matter-of-fact I have. Lieutenant Comberg just left. I overheard him talking to Chief Andrews. He told Andrews that the Captain is getting tired of hearing all the myths, rumors and legends going around the ship. He's told the department heads to bring their departments up to speed on where we're headed and what we'll be doing when we get there.

"Mister Comberg is going to gather us together this afternoon after chow and give us the skinny.

"Meanwhile, I've got a stack of corrections to our pubs that need to be done today."

Message received.

"Hand me the corrections to the Allied Naval Signal Book and I'll get started."

*   *   *

"The Captain has ordered that all departments *not* be fully briefed prior to our getting underway on the day after tomorrow. I can tell you men this much for now: We will be participating in a joint mission with the Air Force for the next three months.

"When we leave Pearl, we'll steam in a south-southwest-erly direction for roughly one thousand miles. This will be the starting point for our exercise.

"Chief Andrews, be sure that your team has the navigation charts that we will need for the mission."

"Yes sir."

"That's all I have for now. Mister Doolen, your division officer, will fully brief all of you after we are underway.

"Alright, let's get busy and get CIC ready to get underway, all pubs and charts corrected and up-to-date, all radars lit off but not energized until we set sea detail, all radar repeaters, IFF, voice radio circuits patched in to proper speakers … you men know the drill."

* * *

"This is the Captain speaking."

Commander William "Bull" Dozier was addressing the crew on the shipboard announcing network:

"Yesterday we got underway from Pearl Harbor and laid in a course for Johnston Atoll, a small Air Force weather station roughly 800 miles in a south-southwesterly direction from Pearl. When we reach our destination, we will then turn to the north-northeast and steam in that direction until reaching French Frigate Shoals, which is the northernmost point of our sector. Having reached that point we'll turn 180 degrees and proceed back to Johnston Atoll, which is the southernmost point of our assigned sector. Upon reaching Johnston Atoll, we will then turn back and head for French Frigate Shoals. And so on, and so on, well you men get the picture.

"We are part of a large task group of destroyers and cruis-ers that are positioned at intervals across the entire Pacific Missile Range. The Air Force, it seems, is developing a new method of recovering important satellites returning from space. We, and other navy ships along the missile range will be pro-viding backup in case we are required to pick up a capsule that the Air Force recovery aircraft has missed. We will see very lit-tle ship traffic, and aircraft entering our assigned sector will be non-existent as they have been warned to steer clear of the range during exercises. In short, we will have very little to do other than our CIC personnel who will be monitoring the telemetering equipment which was installed While we were in Pearl.

"Boredom is the first step toward the decay of safety, which in turn may lead to a serious casualty while we are here. On the other hand, an assignment such as this makes for an excellent opportunity to polish our gunnery skills and reaction time to manning up after an alarm has been sounded. We will polish those skills daily while we are out here.

"Our time out here is also an excellent time to complete those correspondence courses in professional and military skills that are required for promotion.

"That's all for now. If the situation here changes I'll keep you posted."

*   *   *

Radarman First-Class Ron Kivett, the division leading petty officer and second senior enlisted man behind Chief Andrews had placed the CIC team in a three-section underway watch bill. Each section would stand a six-hour watch in CIC with twelve hours off-watch to take care of any ship's work and have time off to relax. While on-watch the men would rotate between, satellite telemetry, navigation, radar monitoring, and radio monitoring, although the reality of our situation was that the chance of responding to any line of sight radio voice transmissions was non-existent as there were simply no other Navy ships within hundreds of miles.

Charlie Floyd's section was midway through another dull afternoon watch. Lieutenant Mandarakis, the ship's gunnery officer, was the CIC Watch Officer for the afternoon watch.

Floyd was having a conversation with the watch officer regarding the capsule recovery procedure.

"Mister M, I'm still not clear on just how the Air Force is going to snag a capsule out of the air.

Mandarakis smiled. "I don't think they are either.

"I Think the way it's supposed to happen is that the Air Force takes a dummy capsule up in one of those U-2 spy planes that has been modified to drop the capsule and jettisons it. The capsule is rigged with a parachute that is deployed when a timer opens the 'chute.

"There is a C-119 box car aircraft flying at a lower altitude that picks up the capsule telemetry and deploys a large net which is lowered from the cargo bay load ramp. The theory is that when the net is trailing at a safe distance behind the aircraft, the net which is anchored by cables from either side of the cargo bay, gently gathers the parachute cords and the capsule is reeled back into the cargo bay. Kind of like trawling for shrimp."

Floyd smiled. "More like trying to catch a nickel thrown from the Empire State Building."

The passageway door to CIC opened and Ron Kivett entered.

"Afternoon, all. Mister M, do you mind if I borrow Floyd for a few minutes? I need to discuss a personnel move with him."

Mandarakis smiled. "I don't know, Kivett, as you can see we are very busy here what with all that's going on."

Kivett smiled and nodded.

"Only be for a couple of minutes. Charlie, come step out on the 01-deck with me for a minute. Or two."

Floyd looked at Lieutenant Mandarakis, who motioned toward the door with glance and the two petty officers exited the door, stepped out on the 01-deck level.

"Shit! Hot out here."

Kivett replied to Floyd's weather report.

"Just be a minute out here. Solomon's been bitching to Mister Doolen that he's getting all the shit jobs and working parties and doesn't have a chance to learn his rate. Says it's holding him back."

"Ron, what's holding him back is that he's dumber than a bag of hammers. The only thing that he's done that is any good is when we send him mess cooking down in the Chief's Mess. They love him down there. Best mess cook they ever had."

"Yeah, well that don't mean shit. Mister Doolen told the Chief who told me to get him up out of berthing compartment cleaning and put him on the watch bill.

"So up he comes, and into your section. Beatty's a short-timer so I'm pulling him from your watch section and putting him in the compartment. Solomon is taking his place in your watch section."

"Jesus, Ron what'd I ever do to you that you're giving me Solomon for Beatty? There are two other sections, you know, why mine?"

"Floyd, you are getting him because you are the junior watch section supervisor and because nobody else would take him. Nurture him, gently train him, make him a valuable member of your team."

"Getting him in my watch section is bad enough. No need for the sarcasm."

*   *   *

The Captain had acquired an orange target buoy with attached radar reflectors from somewhere on the Naval Station in Pearl Harbor for gunnery target practice while we were steaming in our area between Johnston Atoll and French Frigate Shoals. He directed the First Lieutenant, Mister Youmans to secure the buoy on the fantail when not in use as the gunnery target. Whenever he announced a gunnery shoot, Mister Youmans' crew would lower the buoy in the water and the ship would turn and move out to 6000 yards distance from the buoy, present a broadside aspect to the target and have each battery commence firing individually at the buoy. The exercises were designed to develop a competition between the individual gun mount crews to see which mount could come the closest to the target without sinking it. The gun crews themselves tried very hard to sink the damn buoy but they never did; if they sunk the damn thing there'd be no more gunnery exercises.

On occasion, old "Bull" Dozier would have the gunnery department fire a broadside at the target. All three twin 5" 38 caliber mounts and the lone twin 3" 50 caliber mount on the 01-deck aft would unload a salvo in the general direction of the target buoy. Eight naval rifles firing simultaneously, an earth-shattering, ear-splitting, light-bulb popping, overhead dirt-loosing crash that seemed to push the ship several feet in the opposite direction.

When we held one of our frequent gunnery exercises the ship would go to general quarters and secure all doors and hatches to place the ship in a complete water-tight condition. On one of those days that the ship was to fire a broadside, general quarters were called, and the ship went to water-tight status, known as 'Condition Zebra.'

We had been in condition 'Zebra' for some time and Kivett, a chain smoker was dying for a puff or two.

"Hell, we ain't fired yet, probably some problem with one of the mounts. I'm gonna pop out for a quick smoke."

Kivett left CIC, broke water-tight integrity and stepped out on the 01-Deck to light up. He quickly lit a cigarette, took several drags and discarded the remaining butt over the side. As he was opening the passageway door to CIC the broadside let loose.

Wham! Kivett disappeared from the doorway and went flying down the passageway, leaving only the shadow of his ballcap remaining in the doorway for the smallest fraction of a microsecond.

* * *

"Now this is a drill, this is a drill. General Quarters, General Quarters, all hands man your battle stations."

Within minutes CIC was manned up and ready to go.

"Kivett, you want me in the usual place?"

"Right, Bobby, go sit over there on the deck by the gunnery plot. We might need you for a messenger or something."

Bobby Joe Solomon had made the rounds of the various CIC watch stations since returning and had proven adept at screwing up each of them. Whenever there was a gunnery exercise, Kivett had him sit in the corner next to the gunnery officer's station where he'd be out of the way.

"Mind if I shine my shoes while I'm sittin' over there?"

"Go ahead, Bobby, it'll give you something to do while we're doing the shoot."

Solomon went dutifully to his corner section and sat, producing a can of shoe polish. He opened the can and decided to soften the wax by lighting its contents. He held up the can with one hand, lit his Zippo and ignited the wax. The flame from the wax gave off a soft, translucent blue flame, which seemed to briefly mesmerize Solomon.

"YOW!!"

Solomon hadn't considered that the lighted polish in the can would be too hot to hold. He jumped up and let go of the can, sending flaming polish onto his pant leg. The burning polish, which was now released from its can, also found the trouser leg of Lieutenant Mandarakis who jumped up and while attempting to extinguish the flame on his pantleg, knocked over a cold cup of coffee which spilled on the gun plot.

The sound-powered phone talker who had a direct line to the bridge saw the flame and screamed into the speaker, "Fire! Fire in CIC!"

Frank Nash, who heard the sound-powered phone talker's frantic message to the bridge, removed a fire extinguisher from the bulkhead, ran to the fire and delivered the contents of the fire bottle over Lieutenant Mandarakis and Solomon's legs and torso which extinguished the flames.

The Captain, who was on the bridge for the gunnery exercise, heard the fire call from CIC and ordered the Officer of the Deck to "away the fire Party to CIC." Minutes later, the fire party from damage control burst into CIC in full fire dress, with a mountain of fire-fighting equipment at the ready.

Just behind the fire party came one of the ship's hospital corpsmen who treated the two men for minor burns and took them to sick bay for further examination.

The gunnery exercise was canceled for the remainder of the day.

The following day while Lieutenant (junior grade) Doolen was standing the 12 – 16 Officer of the Deck watch on the bridge the ship's executive officer who was on the bridge at the time approached Doolen.

"What the hell happened down there yesterday, Ed?"

Doolen snorted derisively.

"One of my seaman, a sailor named Solomon decided to shine his shoes during GQ. He thought it would be a good idea to soften the polish by lighting it up. The hot tin burned his hand and he threw it down which set his and Jim's pant leg on fire. Everything went downhill after that."

"And this sailor is a CIC watchstander?"

Doolen shook his head.

"Sent him mess cooking this morning. He's as dumb as a bag of hammers."

* * *

USS Ernest G. Small

A Hard Landing

Pernod. My old man used to call it "Panther Piss," and that referred to the stuff that was imported for American consumption. European pernod was said to contain an added ingredient, I'm not sure what, maybe some narcotic of some sort or something else that was supposed to affect your inhibitions. Some said that it had the same effect as the Greek Ouzo, the European version of which was also supposed to have been banned for sale and consumption in the States. I don't believe any of that.

*   *   *

Summer, 1964

I was having a smoke on the empty gun sponson across the passageway from CIC and chatting with Chief Charlie Early. Charlie was the division leading chief for OI Division aboard the aircraft carrier *Franklin D. Roosevelt*. The sea and anchor detail, which had been called away while the ship navigated to her deep-water anchorage 3000 yards outside the Cannes, France inner harbor, had just been secured.

"Been here before?"

I nodded. "Two years ago, on the *Nantahala*. Cannes is my favorite Mediterranean port.

"Can't compare with the ports in Wespac, though."

Charlie Early shrugged. "Can't say one way or another. I've always been an east coast sailor.

"Chief, are you headed over on the beach later?"

"Yeah, I'm gonna put on some civvies and head over later, grab a nice French dinner in some classy restaurant and hit a few night clubs, then head on back to the ship.

"What about you?"

"As soon as I finish this cigarette I'm headed for the compartment to put my whites on and catch the liberty launch to fleet landing and head up the hill to *Bistro Roger*."

Early shook his head.

"Never heard of it. Is it near the waterfront?"

"Uh Uh. Up the hill about a mile or more from the waterfront, mostly locals and a few sailors that know about it. Owned by a guy and his family, nothing special about it – except for Monique."

I didn't mind sharing my information with the chief as I knew him to be not only a career sailor, but a career "brown-bagger" as well. You know, the kind of guy who brings his lunch that was packed by his wife to the ship every day when we are in port in the States. Charlie Early was as married as anyone could possibly be, a man who both loved and respected his wife and family, the kind of guy that would break out the family photos from his wallet at the drop of a hat.

Charlie Early gave me a disapproving look.

"I don't even want to know about this Monique. I need no further explanation to know that she is a prostitute."

I smiled, winked and re-cycled my eyebrows.

"Really, Chief, you didn't think that I was headed up that hill to ask Roger how his family was doing, did you?"

Early rewarded my sarcasm with a wry smile.

"I have only known you for the three short months that you have been aboard, but that has been enough time to know that you were going ashore to look for love or whatever love passes for over here.

"Well, you're one-and-twenty so you don't need any morality lectures from me. You wouldn't listen if I tried."

I smiled and gave him a quick shrug.

"Sailor, keep in mind that you need to be on the first launch heading into fleet landing tomorrow morning. Don't miss it and above all, don't miss the van going to the airport. The Marines aren't going to hold that C-130 just for you."

"My seabag is already packed, Chief, and my dress canvas is ready to go. I'll be up at 0500, quick dance in the splash locker, shave, dress and head for the afterbrow in plenty of time to make the launch."

*　　*　　*

Bistro Roger hadn't changed since my last visit two years in the past. The cigarette and scratch-off lottery counter was just inside the door to the right, an extension of the service bar which ran the length of the café. The back bar was completely mirrored which lent depth to the overall feeling of the room and had liquor and liqueur bottles flanking an espresso machine. Along the front of the opposite wall were a few booths, the seats of which were covered with red vinyl. A few two-top tables completed the décor. Roger was working behind the bar while Mrs. Roger and the two little Rogers occupied a booth, both children engaged in finishing their lessons for the following day.

One customer sat at the bar, busily engaged with Roger in a conversation about what I later learned was about the local soccer, or more appropriately, football (I was in France, after all) team.

I took a stool midway along the bar and sat down. Roger, who noticed me out of the corner of his eye, abruptly broke off the conversation and walked down to where I was seated.

Good morning, M'sieu, what may I serve you?"

I smiled and replied, "Good morning, Roger, I'd like a pernod and water, please. First one today."

Roger nodded and moved to the area where the bottle was located, retrieved a glass from the back bar, added a couple of ice cubes from the ice machine and poured a healthy shot of the liquid over the cubes. He then filled a small carafe with water from the tap and placed both the glass and carafe in front of me. I poured a bit of water from the carafe into the glass containing the pernod, watching the mixture assume a pleasant chartreuse-milky color, placed a100-Franc note on the bar and raised my glass in a small toast.

"Tchin-tchin, Roger."

The familiar licorice-like taste warmed my inside and after only one moderate-sized sip began to relax me. The last at-sea period had been grueling. We had lost a man overboard and had one casualty following another.

Roger nodded, smiling, Ah, M'sieu, you have been to France before?"

"Oui, in fact I have been here to your café before. Two years ago, when my ship, the *Nantahala* paid a port visit to Cannes."

Roger was busily searching his memory bank, to no avail.

"Ah, well welcome back, *mon ami!* We are very glad that you have remembered."

Roger looked over at Mrs. Roger and inquired:

"Vous souvenez-vous de ce marin qui était ici avant?"

I had a feeling that Roger's remark to his wife concerned me. I turned to face her.

Mrs. Roger was studying me as if she were trying to think of something from the past. Then, suddenly she remembered. Her face brightened.

"Ah! Oui! Il était là tous les jours pour passer du temps avec Monique. Elle l'aimait beaucoup, si innocente, si jeune."

I wasn't altogether sure what Mrs. Roger had replied, but I was certain that it had something to do with Monique.

"My wife remembers you, m'sieu. She said that you were here every day to spend time with Monique, n'est ce pas?"

"Yes, that's right, and while we're on the subject has she come down from the apartment yet?

Roger shook his head.

"No, no not yet. We don't see her, usually before lunch. If you want, I'll call her now."

"No, that's okay, I'll wait. Looks like there's a hole in the bottom of the glass, Roger. Pour me another, please and let me try some of those pastries."

*　　*　　*

Two hours passed while waiting for Monique to appear. Roger had gone back to arguing football with the Frenchman at the end of the bar, occasionally interrupting his conversation to provide me with another drink. I was feeling very little pain when the door to the upstairs apartment opened and Monique entered to have her lunch. Roger pointed to me and began to speak in French."

"Monique, vous souvenez-vous de ce marin d'il y a deux ans? Il est revenu pour vous rendre visite à nouveau."

She was as strikingly lovely as I remembered her; a tall, leggy, thirty-five or so redhead, with sparkling green eyes and lovely straight teeth, mother of a teenager that she was working to put through private school. God, it was so good to see her again!

Monique looked in my direction. I put on my very best 5-pernod smile.

"Ah, oui, oui! You wrote some letters to me after you left, no? Wait a moment... Bobby! I called you Bobby. Yes! You came back to see me, did you?"

"I nodded my head vigorously. "Monique, who *wouldn't* come back to see you?"

Monique threw her head back and gave a short laugh. "Yes, that is right! Who *wouldn't* come back to see me?

"Bobby, I am going out for lunch. Why don't you come with me? Later I can show you my new furniture and wall decorations. Would you like that, yes?"

I was grinning so hard my jaw was beginning to ache.

"I would like that, yes, and I would love to buy you lunch."

"Well then, let us go, ma jeune amant."

After lunch, we spent the afternoon in her apartment talking and making love accompanied by a bottle of pernod. Her wall decorations and furniture were very nice indeed. I loved what she had done with the bedroom.

* * *

The early evening had arrived by the time I left Monique, a nearly empty bottle of pernod and most of my francs. Rather than wait for a cab I decided to walk back to the waterfront and part with my remaining francs in one of the sailor bars that were within a few blocks of fleet landing. Truth be known a walk of a mile or so would help to clear my head of some of the "panther piss" soaking my brain.

I arrived at the waterfront and turned in to the first saloon I saw. Crowded with drunk sailors and bar girls it was a far cry from where I had recently been. I looked around the room and saw three of my division mates, Chief Charlie Early, Radarman First E.J. Atwood and Radarman Second Matt Perry at a table near the back. Perry was motioning for me to join them.

The waitress arrived as I sat down, and I ordered a pernod and water.

Atwood, the son of an Oklahoma oil field roughneck, and a fanatic Oklahoma Sooner football fan was the first to speak.

"What the fuck is up with you gettin' a set of orders after bein' here only three fuckin' months? You got pull or somethin'? I been tryin' to get off this bucket for over a year."

"E.J., if I knew any more about it I'd be happy to tell you. All I know is I'm supposed to report to the North American Aviation plant in Columbus, Ohio in 14 days. The only thing other than that is that after I leave there I'm supposed to go to a Heavy Attack Squadron in Florida somewhere."

"Well it looks to me, Charlie Early opined, "That you must be a part of some highly classified operation that's going down and they need a radarman with a high security clearance."

"I don't know any more about it that you guys do, nobody on the ship or air wing knows anything either. I'll know when I know is all I can say."

The evening moved along with my "one or two drinks before I go back and get a good night's sleep" rapidly disappearing. At about 2200 Atwood had an idea.

"Sittin' around here's gettin' old. Let's hit one more bar before we head back to the ship."

Atwood looked to Chief Early for agreement.

"Why not? Let's go."

We all got up and left the bar, turned toward the waterfront and turned again at the intersection. Atwood looked in all directions to see if there was a bar that looked inviting.

I was feeling really, *really* on top of the world, ready for anything, charged up about the mysterious set of orders.

Atwood's booze radar had a contact.

"Look down the street, that big sign that says, "Moulin Rouge." Looks like a good place for last call."

We turned and walked the half-block to the entrance. E.J. and I walked in first, followed by Charlie Early and Perry. The outside door opened into a small vestibule which led through to a second inner door to the bar. In the vestibule stood two tough looking characters.

"No! No! Can't come in this bar for, it for officers only."

I'm not exactly certain why, but the greasy looking Frog that tried to stop us pissed me off.

"Bullshit!"

I began to push my way toward the inner door. I didn't like the way the Frog at the door spoke to me, and neither did the pernod sloshing around inside me. The Frog with the big mouth started pushing me back toward the outer door while the second Frog produced a sap from his pocket and started hitting me on the top of my head. I let fly with what must have been the best left hook that I have ever thrown and hit Frog One right on the button! Frog One staggered back, hit the inner door and went down. When the inner door gave way to Frog One's backward falling body I briefly saw some officers in civilian clothes at the bar accompanied by some really hot looking women, not the kind that you would see in our sailor joints. About this time old E.J. Atwood, who would often regale us with his feats from his high school football days when he was "filling the air with footballs," filled the air with lefts and rights in Frog Two's direction. Frog Two hit the deck next to Frog One.

By this time everyone at the bar was screaming for the Shore Patrol and the Gendarmes. I turned around to see Charlie Early heading down the street at lightning speed. I suppose he was worried about being busted back to First Class and I certainly had no cause to fault him for that.

Not only that, if his wife found out about his behavior, she'd kill him!

E.J. suggested that we get the hell out of there and we did just that, leaving Frogs One and Two on the deck. I went straight back to fleet landing to wait for the next launch back to the ship to get some sleep before the plane trip in the morning. It was 2330 on the night before my flight.

* * *

0500 arrives much too soon on a hangover morning, which made me something less than pleasant when the messenger of the watch shined his flashlight in my face and shook my shoulder.

"Wake up, sailor, it's 0500 and I'm not coming back to see if you're out of your rack."

I was not in the best of spirits.

"Nobody asked you to. Now get that flashlight out of my face before I stick it up your ass."

The messenger laughed. "Not a morning person, are we?"

I crawled out of my bunk with a splitting headache. I smoothed my hair ... "OW! What the fuck?"

Then I remembered: the Frog with the sap. There had to be at least a half-dozen, maybe more small knots all over the top of my skull. I grabbed my towel hanging from the bunk chain and staggered into the head for a shower. Today was going to be a *very, very* long day.

*   *   *

The Marine Corps C-130 put the wheels in the well at precisely 0834, climbed to altitude, and set a westerly course toward the sprawling naval base at Rota. The flight would take approximately three and one-half hours. The web seats were lined along each side of the cargo compartment and occupied by seventy Marines in full combat gear. I stood out like a sore thumb, sitting in one of the cargo net seats in my dress canvas, hugging my seabag, vowing to the Deity that if he'd help me with this hangover I'd do the next one on my own.

When the aircraft had reached its assigned flight level, the gunny sergeant loadmaster handed me a box lunch for the trip.

"Here you go, sailor. Complements of the United States Marine Corps."

I took the box lunch but wasn't sure if I'd be able to eat anything from it.

"Where are these guys headed, Gunny? Looks like they're loaded for bear."

I had to speak loudly to be heard over the growl of the four Allison T-56 turboprops. His voice sounded to me as if my ears were waterlogged.

"Headed for a staging area at Cubi in the P.I., next stop Da Nang. Looks like things are heating up over there in Veet-naam. Advance element of the First Marines. Gonna kick ass and take names. Where you goin'?"

"Not with them, although I'd like to be back in the P.I. for sure. Headed Stateside for new orders."

"Well, good luck with that, sailor. We'll be in Rota in a couple of hours."

"Thanks, Gunny. Best to you guys, too."

'Wonder how long I'll be in Rota?'

The monotonous hum of the turboprops steered me into a light doze, falling in and out of a twilight-like consciousness. The hum and whine of the turboprops had a mesmerizing effect.

"Strap in, sailor. We're on final into Rota."

It seemed like it had only been ten minutes or so since I dozed off.

"Right. I'm awake, Gunny."

I fumbled around, looking for and eventually locating both ends of the web seat restraint, and I strapped myself in. A Marine corporal seated next to me handed me my white hat.

"Here's your speed ring, sailor boy. You dropped it while you were sleeping.

"Thanks, I...."

WHAM! The big Hercules met the runway with a tremendous impact, sending loose gear flying hazardously about and throwing the gunny on his back and toward the rear cargo ramp.

"Son of a bitch! Who....what...did we crash?"

The Marine corporal's eyes were the size of two large doorknobs.

The loadmaster quickly picked himself up and put on the intercom headset.

"Major, what the fuck was that? Uh huh. Uh huh. Roger."

The gunny switched on the cargo mike.

"The co-pilot landed a little hard, and we've blown at least one tire on the main landing gear. Might be a bit bumpy until we stop. If you see me drop the cargo door and haul ass, then you better haul ass with me. If you see me open the cargo door and start to secure the bay, wait for your captain to disembark you in an orderly fashion."

The lumbering Hercules, so smooth and steady in flight, bumped and jounced and creaked its way to its assigned place on the tarmac, finally coming to an embarrassed halt. Gunny unsecured and lowered the cargo ramp while the Marine officer and first sergeant formed up their men and led them out into the late morning sun of Rota, Spain.

I was the last to leave the aircraft.

"Thanks for the ride, Gunny. Hope your next landing is a better one."

"Can't get but a little worse, sailor. Wherever you're going, good luck!"

*   *   *

Photo # NH 97756 Sailors from USS Greenwich Bay on the French Riviera in 1961

Cannes liberty

The Interior Design Consultant

It's kind of like going on a trip and while you are away, your family moves out-of-state and doesn't leave a forwarding address.

*   *   *

Late Spring, 1971

I left the Naval Air Station in Sanford, Florida in the fall of 1965, headed for Alameda, California to join the *USS Ranger*. *Ranger*, in turn was about to get underway for the South China Sea to join the Navy's Seventh Fleet. She and her embarked Air Group 14 were going to provide air support for ground forces engaged in the war in South Vietnam, and later provide air strikes on ground targets in North Vietnam as part of the "Rolling Thunder" bombing campaign.

We would be gone for eight months before returning to our home port in Alameda, but I wasn't particularly keen on returning with her. I had become quite friendly with a seventeen-year-old girl who worked in one of the myriad bars and nightclubs in the Philippine town of Olongapo City, and as a result I was looking for a way to stay in Southeast Asia.

That opportunity presented itself in July of 1966 when Seventh Fleet sent a message calling for volunteers to "cross-deck" from *Ranger* to her relief carrier *USS Constellation*, which was scheduled to arrive during the first week of August. I volunteered, was given the go-ahead and on August 6th I checked in to the air ops office with bag and baggage, boarded the "Jolly Green Giant" Navy helicopter that would ferry roughly a dozen or so of the officers and enlisted men that had volunteered for the "exchange of Yankee Team Assets from *Ranger* to the *Constellation* which was patiently waiting on the horizon.

Most of the next four years were spent in Southeast Asia.

*   *   *

After four years in the Western Pacific, cross-decking to different large deck aircraft carriers and one final year in-country

Vietnam tour as the only radarman aboard a 220-ton patrol gunboat, I received orders to a reconnaissance squadron that was very much the same as the squadron that I was attached to in Sanford back in 1964. Reconnaissance Wing One, when the closure of the Sanford Naval Air Station was imminent, had relocated to the now vacant Turner Air Force Base in Albany, Georgia – the very heart of the "Red Clay" district in Central Georgia. I wasn't all that thrilled about the Wing location. Central Georgia? Not for me, but as they say, "Orders is orders."

I checked in with the Squadron at Albany and was assigned a barracks room in the former Air Force barracks. It was the nicest barracks I'd ever seen. My roommate was a first-class aviation boatswain by the name of Coats. Coats sported a huge handlebar moustache that was the envy of moustache aficionados everywhere. He was a good guy to room with as he was almost never around. I had the room pretty much to myself which after eight months of being stacked up like a sardine in the Carrier crew's berthing and the cramped gunboat sleeping area was a real treat.

There was nothing for me to do now that the Squadron had left the Carrier and was back at Albany as the squadron wasn't flying electronic reconnaissance missions. The Squadron wasn't quite sure what to do with me until word came down from the Wing that we had to provide a senior petty officer for Shore Patrol duty.

Guess who got the job?

I really didn't mind all that much. I was given Temporary Assigned Duty orders to report in to the huge Marine Corps Supply Center which was also located in Albany. I was assigned to the Provost Marshal's Office within the Center, reporting directly to the First Sergeant. I was assigned a desk within the office and would be patrolling with a Staff Sergeant, picking up and returning prisoners from the City Jail to their respective commands. It was terrific duty, on for twenty-four hours and off for the next seventy-two.

When my ninety-day tour was up I asked to be assigned another tour and as the Squadron had no objection and the Marines didn't either, I turned around and went right back to work conducting jail sweeps. My thoughts were that the second tour would carry me right through to my shore duty orders which were due in any day. The only embarrassing moment in the job was when I had to pick up Red Powell, a mustang Navy Lieutenant who was officer in charge of the Base rolling stock and fuel farm. I knew Red from my road running days at Sanford and liked him. He was a hard drinker and a great guy to work for according to his Chiefs and Petty Officers. Red had gotten into a bit of trouble in town - the locals never really had warmed up to the Navy - and had gotten himself thrown in jail. I was making the hourly sweep with the Staff Sergeant and walked into the Albany Police cellblock and heard:

"Nasty, goddam, son I'm glad to see you!"

I knew that gravelly voice immediately. It was Lieutenant Red Powell who was calling me from the jail drunk tank.

"Goddam, Red, what the hell have you gotten into in town?"

"Nasty, see if you can fix this. I'm in hot water with the base commander as it is."

I looked at the Marine and he shrugged. I went to the desk sergeant and asked if we could somehow let old Red off the hook. I may have embellished a bit by saying that he'd never recovered fully from a rocket attack in Da Nang back in1968 and sometimes drank a bit too much to forget the experience.

Embellish, hell! What I did was flat out lie through my teeth. Old Red hadn't been west of New Orleans since Korea. My plea fell on deaf ears. Apparently, Red had been hauled in on a DUI and that was one offense that wasn't about to be swept under the rug. He was there for the night and wouldn't be released until he made an appearance in front of a magistrate late the next morning.

That was the last time I ever saw Red Powell. Several years after the incident Red passed away. I regret not being able to help him that night.

* * *

The Air Force really knows how to make a life in the service comfortable for the troops. Every building, office, recreational facility, even the medical dispensary was the best there was to offer. The Sanford base, by comparison seemed primitive. While I didn't get too see all that many of the buildings on the base, I was living in one of the enlisted barracks that was the most comfortable barracks that I'd ever experienced.

The one thing that Albany didn't have, though, was good liberty. The town was seeded with retired Air Force types that didn't like the base closure one bit. They liked the Navy's take-over of the former SAC Base even less.

I began spending more of my free time at the base Acey-Deucy Club after meeting and dating the club secretary, Linda. That will be another story for another time.

The Club had originally been built when the Air Force had occupied the field and it was a top shelf affair with a large restaurant and bar area with a band platform. Off to the side and toward the back was a small stag bar that was a "dirty shirt" affair. Sailors would often hit the stag bar in their working uniforms which weren't allowed in the club proper.

The stag bar was also the repository for the heavy drinkers. Someone from the cleaning staff would unlock the side door entrance to the stag bar every morning at around 0700 for anyone who might need a little taste to get them over the night before. As there was no bartender on duty - the club hadn't officially opened yet - a large empty beer pitcher was placed on the bar the night before. Anyone stopping in on the way to work would simply abide by the honor system and put the money for the drink in the pitcher. When the bar opened at 1130 that morning for lunch the bartender would take the money in the pitcher and ring it up.

One of the stag bar's best customers was a first-class avionics technician named Ed Farley. Ed realized that he was never going to be selected for promotion to chief petty officer and that suited him just fine. Ed had a clerical job in the avionics shop, one that didn't require much initiative. That also suited him just fine. Ed was biding his time, drinking his way toward retirement and bothering no one. Ed would show up at 0700 in the morning to contribute to the honor system, go to work until lunch, return to the stag bar at lunch time for a ninety-minute bracer or three, and reappear again at 1600 for some serious elbow bending, pouring himself out at closing time to wobble to his barracks room for a bit of sleep before the process was repeated the next day.

Club management had lobbied for funding to replace the worn and dirty carpeting in the stag bar and when the money was finally released Ed McKellar, the assistant manager decided to allow the patrons to decide by selecting one of the many sample carpet patches attached to a ring. Majority would decide. The most number of picks of a certain sample would win the day and that would be the carpet design that would be installed.

The poll of the patrons continued over several days. When the sample ring was given to Ed Farley one evening at around 2200, he selected each individual sample, placing each one on the bar, one sample at a time and banging his head on the sample.

McKellar, who was standing behind Farley while all of this was going, was puzzled.

"What the hell do you think you're doing, Farley? Hurry up and make a pick."

Farley turned around to look at McKellar.

"Take it easy, McKellar, I'm making my selection just like everyone else.

When I fall off this stool at closing time I want a soft landing."

*　*　*

A Navy RA-5C flies over NAS Albany

Part Two
Really Short Stories

Whiskey Bill Drops His Tool Bag

Autumn, 1970. Sydney, Australia.
Aboard USS America
Our last stop before returning to the States via the Drake passage and Rio de Janeiro was Sydney, Australia. My recon squadron was all but done flying and our squadron skipper, Commander Bill Laurentis had instructed his various departments to grant maximum liberty. Dick Shore, the squadron personnelman, Bill "Whiskey Bill" Thompson, the squadron lead parachute rigger and Ken "Willie" Williamson and I took some leave and caught the first available liberty boat ashore. Once ashore Dick, Bill, Willie and I rented a room in the Texas Tavern Hotel which was in Sydney's "gut," Kings Cross. We were planning to use the room as a base of operations to change clothes and have the occasional nap when the strong Aussie beer or other spirits overtook us. Willie, never much of a drinker, spent most of his time sightseeing while Shore, Thompson and I did some major pub crawling.

The Kings Cross bars along the streets near the hotel had touts outside pitching the merits of the "lovely" girls and the drink prices inside. Some of them even had coupons for free drinks. We hit a few of these joints and were quite disappointed. The reality was nowhere near what the pitchman outside was describing. Ever the wag, Dick Shore quipped, "How do you like that! The guy outside tells us that there's over fifty women inside. We go in and there's four women who are all over fifty." After a night or two of hitting the joints we decided to confine our lounge crawling evenings to the cellar bar at the hotel.

Bill Thompson did not acquire the "Whiskey Bill" nickname by accident. When his ship would announce liberty call Thompson was usually off the ship headed for the first saloon that he came across. His beverage of choice was the boilermaker, a large shot of straight whiskey – it didn't matter to him which brand – chased by a glass of whatever beer happened to be on tap. By the time Bill arrived at his fourth bar of the day he was carrying what my old man used to call "a real package" of booze and was ready for any eventuality.

Bill never drew a sober breath the whole time that we were in Sydney. His morning routine consisted of a pull or two from the whiskey bottle he had bought and kept in the room for "medicinal purposes." This morning routine gave him the courage to face the world. After showering and dressing, another pull or two from the "duty whiskey bottle" gave him the fortitude to square up with the day's drinking that was certain to come.

It will come as no surprise to anyone to learn that Thompson stayed loaded the whole time that we were in Sydney. After his morning "medicine" he'd venture from the hotel in search of a bar that had opened early and often would find one. By the time that noon rolled around he'd return to the hotel room for a nap, after which he'd join the throng at the hotel cellar bar at around 1600 hours and begin the next round of drinking.

Shore and I were sitting at the hotel cellar bar the night before the ship was to get underway for the trip back to the States via the Drake Passage, the always storm-ravaged and dangerous body of water between the southernmost tip of the South American continent and Antarctica. We had both packed our bags and were ready to get back to the ship somewhat earlier than usual to be clear-headed and ready to sail. Just as we were about to leave, Thompson sailed down the steps to the bar and sat down next to us. He was already, to borrow a phrase, "three sheets to the wind."

That didn't stop him from ordering a drink for the three of us. The bartender looking him over, decided that he'd seen drunker people belly up to his bar – but not many – and decided to fill the order.

"Couple more and I'm headed back to the ship," he announced. "Had a great time on the strip this afternoon, fell in love twice."

Dick Shore laughed. "More like in heat. I'm surprised that you could fall anywhere but on your drunk-ass face."

"Is that so," Thompson replied, "well let me tell you all about it after I make a head call."

Thompson got up from his seat and was preparing to weave his way through the crowded-to capacity bar and lounge to the stairs which led to the men's room in the lobby when Dick Shore grabbed his arm and whispered in his ear.

"Bill, you haven't got a hair on your ass if you don't moon the crowd here when you get to the top of the stairs."

Parachute Rigger First-Class William "Whiskey Bill" Thompson drew himself up to his full 5' 9" height, cocked his head to one side, grinned, replied, "Is that so? Watch and learn, shipmate." and headed unsteadily for the steps.

When he reached the top step, Thompson dropped his trousers and skivvies, turned, bent over and whistled as loud as he knew how. Everyone in the lounge looked in the direction of the whistle and were afforded a clear view of Thompson's stern sheets.

Shore had an evil grin on his face. He shouted at the top of his lungs, "Look out Bill, they threw a snake right behind you!"

Thompson wheeled around suddenly to see where the snake was located, giving everyone in the lounge a clear view of his uncovered toolbag.

Much to old Whiskey Bill's dismay and to our delight there wasn't a scream or gasp to be heard. There was only the sound of amused laughter. The bartender, who was the only person in the lounge who was not amused, notified the bouncer who unceremoniously collared old Whiskey Bill and waltzed him through the hotel lobby to the front door and deposited him on the sidewalk.

*   *   *

Street scene, Kings Cross, Sydney Australia

O'Malley's Emergency

My second tour of shore duty began in the summer of 1971 when, after almost four years of different operations and ships in Southeast Asia, I received orders to the Recruit Training Command at the recently established Naval Training Center in Orlando, Florida. I was to spend the next three years of my life as a recruit company commander, training groups of new recruits in the basics of navy life at sea and instilling a sense of teamwork in them. Bottom line: every few months I'd be given charge of 67 young men from different parts of the country with vastly different backgrounds whose idea of working as a team was as remote to most of them as was the chance of flying to Mars. My job was to take charge of a bunch of teenagers whose idea of marching as a unit was akin to herding cats, and in nine weeks' time have them squared away and marching smartly in step, eager to report to their first tour of sea duty.

*   *   *

Winter, 1972
My third recruit company was, I believe to this day, assembled by the Deity to punish me for all my past transgressions. They just couldn't seem to adapt to a military environment. There always seemed to be one recruit that would have his barracks locker fouled up, or have a shoelace untied at morning parade inspection, or couldn't remember one of the general orders when asked by an inspector during an inspection. The Company's performance during the first four weeks of their training cycle – the basic weeks when marching, general orders, proper locker stowage and other functions designed to get them thinking as a unit - kept us in the lower end of our training group. During those four weeks I was hardly ever at home. Thank heaven there was a bunk in my barracks office!

We somehow managed to stumble through the basic training side of the schedule and were ready for the advanced training which consisted mainly of classroom work and simulated shipboard watch-standing aboard the ship mockup, the *USS*

Recruit, a scaled-down wooden building built in the likeness of a navy destroyer escort.

The Saturday before the shift from basic to advanced training was designated as a recruit liberty day, a day when the company recruits would vote to visit a local tourist attraction. Company Commanders were required to "chaperone" the recruits for their liberty day. I invited my girlfriend to join me for the recruit Saturday liberty day.

The company chose Disney World as the attraction that they would visit for their first Navy liberty. A chartered bus picked us up and transported us to Disney World where my young charges were free to visit the various attractions either singly or with a few of their company buddies. When the bus arrived at the Disney World parking lot I gathered them around, gave them the list of "dos and don'ts and told them when to be back at the bus for the trip back to the base. They all indicated that they understood, I gave them one last reminder about getting into trouble and off they went, determined to enjoy their only day off in more than four weeks. My girlfriend and I boarded the monorail for the Contemporary Hotel where we would have lunch, shop and generally rubberneck around the Magic Kingdom until it was time to go back to the bus and get a head count before busing back to the barracks.

The designated time to board the bus arrived and my head count showed that two recruits were missing.

The driver approached me and asked about leaving the theme park.

"What do you want me to do?"

"Let's wait an extra thirty minutes and if these two clowns aren't back by then we'll head back to the base without them."

My recruit chief petty officer, who ran the company in my absence had taken a head count. The two missing recruits were Milton O'Malley and a young recruit with a chip on his shoulder named Freeman.

The extra half hour came and went, and when the two missing recruits didn't show up we headed back to the barracks. Upon returning I went directly to Regimental HQ to report them as AWOL only to find them waiting for me there complete with two arrest reports. It seems that O'Malley and Freeman had approached a civilian in one of the men's rooms and asked him to buy some beer for them! The "civilian" turned out to be a Disney World security officer who detained them and summoned the police, who arrested them and brought them back to the Recruit Command. Lieutenant Moriarty, the Regimental Commander was considering sending the two to the Military Indoctrination Company, an intensive training company for recruits that were oblivious to standard discipline, for a week of punishment drill.

"Well, Mister Stockton, the police have found your two strays. They were trying to buy beer in a men's room located in the Contemporary Hotel… from a hotel security guard!

"Buying beer when you are underage is one thing but trying to buy beer from the security guard! How in the world have these two clowns managed to get this far along in training without being shown the gate, that's what I want to know?"

I could see a storm brewing on the horizon.

"Sir it is no secret that neither of these two are Rhodes Scholars, that is for sure. Do you want to set them back to begin basic again?"

Upon hearing this Milton O'Malley jumped up, waving his arms.

"Wait! I signed up with my brother John. Our recruiter guaranteed that we'd go through boot camp together!"

I gave O'Malley my "keep your damn boot mouth shut" look.

Lieutenant O'Malley was late for his dinner at home with his wife and consequently was not in a good mood.

"Which one are you, O'Malley or Freeman?"

"O'Malley," came the reply.

"O'Malley, SIR, clown. Did your recruiter tell you that the two of you would stay together if one of you was a clown who couldn't follow instructions?"

Moriarty turned to me with a question.

"Mister Stockton, what kind of recruit is this clown's brother shaping up to be?"

"Quiet, squared away, no problem at all, Mister Moriarty."

Moriarty thought for a moment, then rendered his decision.

"Right. Here's what we're going to do. We are going to send you two to the Military Indoctrination Company Barracks for one week of very, very intensive training. Should either of you cause any trouble over there, even the slightest trouble I will set you back to a beginning training group and you will begin the basic training four weeks again.

"If after one week you two haven't made any waves over there you will return to Mister Stockton's Company to complete your advanced training.

"Mister Stockton, march these two over to the MIC Barracks. They are expected."

"Aye, aye sir. You two hit the grinder and fall in a single line."

The two recruits scrambled out of the regiment office. Moriarty indicated that he wanted a word.

"If those two make it through MIC and come back to you, keep up the pressure. They will either sink or swim."

* * *

After one week of "intensive training" in the MIC Barracks Freeman and O'Malley were happy to get back with the company and pick up where they left off. Freeman was a changed recruit, a model for the others to follow. O'Malley, whose performance had improved some, was beginning to show a bit of the Irish leprechaun from time to time, but still had trouble with uniform and barracks inspections. I was becoming really frustrated with his constant gigs for irish pennants hanging loose from his uniforms and locker inspection gigs.

One Saturday morning after O'Malley had hit a quinella – failed a locker inspection and was gigged for irish pennants protruding from his dungaree trousers I ordered him to don his wool watch cap, blue working jacket and leggings and took him to the barracks boiler room where it had to be at least twenty degrees hotter than the squad bay. With his wool watch cap pulled over his ears and jacket buttoned up to his neck I initiated a series of jumping jacks which I periodically paused to have him recite his general orders. This bit of remedial instruction continued for about thirty minutes until O'Malley's face assumed a reddish hue.

"Alright, O'Malley, loosen your jacket, get back up to the squad bay and prepare for a locker and bunk inspection in fifteen minutes.

"Get some water to rehydrate."

O'Malley gasped something that sounded remotely like "okay" and wobbled up the ladder to the second-floor squad bay.

He passed the re-inspection with flying colors.

"Now you see how squared away you can be when you are motivated to do so.

"*Well done*, O'Malley. I don't think that I've ever put those two words together and hooked them up with your name, have I?"

"Don't think so, sir."

"Alright then, go into the lounge area and sit on your ass for a while until we march over for chow."

O'Malley headed for the couch in the lounge area while I went into my office, closed the door and began working on the following week's schedule.

About an hour or so after O'Malley's specialized instruction and re-inspection of his locker and bunk area I was still in my office working when I heard a knock on the office door. It was Milton O'Malley. The dialogue exchange went something like:

Me: "Enter."

O: "Sir, Seaman Recruit O'Malley reporting as ordered, sir."

Me: "What are your orders?"

O: "Sir, request permission to go to Sick Bay, sir."

At this point I began to think that our extra instruction period in the boiler room had caused some sort of physical injury to the kid and if that's the case my fifteen-year Navy career is over. I decided to proceed cautiously.

Me: "I see. You do understand that normal Sick Bay hours are from 0800 to 1600 Monday through Friday. Outside of those hours are reserved for emergencies only. You DO understand that, O'Malley?"

At this point I was beginning to sweat.

O: "Sir, yes sir."

Me: "Very well. We'll get you over there right away. We'll take my car. What is the nature of your Sick Bay complaint?"

I took a deep breath and waited for O'Malley's reply.

O: "Sir, I have really bad …. acne, sir."

Me: "O'Malley…. Ah, hell. Get the fuck out of my office right after you drop and give me twenty."

O (smiling): "Sir, yes sir."

I'm almost certain that I saw a smirk on O'Malley's acne-decorated face.

Maybe the kid will make a good sailor yet.

* * *

Recruit Training Command Orlando, Florida

Jack Morgenstern's
Final Resting Place

I seem to have acquired this curiosity somewhere along the way. A curiosity that has me surfing the internet whenever I think of friends and shipmates that I have known at one time or another during the 60-plus years that have gone by since I first raised my right hand in an oath of allegiance just before boarding a train bound for Chicago and service in the Navy. Last week it was Jack Morgenstern's turn. Jack died at 58 in his adopted home town of Sanford.

* * *

Winter, 1964
I exited the Trailways Bus at the station in Sanford, Florida. The sun was shining brightly and the last vestiges of the flu-like cold that I picked up while on leave back in New Jersey was reluctantly fading away. Looking around the town I noticed a turn-of-the-century design hotel, the Valdez Hotel. If there is a hotel, I reasoned, there must be a restaurant inside. I took charge of my luggage and crossed the street, entering the hotel. I passed the vacant registration desk and walked into an area whose signage read "Caribe Lounge," noticing that the wooden floors groaned and creaked as I crossed the lobby. It was obvious that the hotel had served the community for at least a half-century, probably more.

The lounge had a full bar and several tables along the side wall. The door to the hotel parking lot was located at the end of the row of tables. A door behind the bar opened into the kitchen. There were several people having lunch at the tables. One person, a man, sat at the bar with a mixed drink in front of him. I took a seat at the bar.

"You here for the Navy?" The man at the bar was speaking to me. I turned to get a better look at the man.

"Yes, I'm here for my two-year tour of shore duty."

The man appeared to be in his early to mid-forties, medium height with a craggy, ruddy complexion. He had a thick, full head of dark-red hair cut in a flattop. Smiling, he reached into the pocket of his short-sleeved dress shirt, retrieved a business card, smiled, and handed it to me.

"Jack Morgenstern. I'm a sales executive for Holler Chevrolet here in town. "Hard to get around down here in Central Florida without a car. Bus service doesn't exist, and the cabs are pretty scarce, too. How about a drink?"

'What the hell', I thought. 'Sun's already over the yardarm.'

"Why not? I'll have a Bacardi and Coke."

"Dawn, a Bacardi and Coke for this young sailor who has just arrived for duty at the air base. Welcome to Sanford, sailor."

Dawn, the day bartender, mixed the drink and brought it to me.

"Welcome to Sanford. I'm Dawn. Where are you coming from?"

"Thank you, Dawn. Coming from a carrier in the Med via the North American Aviation plant in Columbus. I'll be here for two years."

"Well, glad to have you with us. You will find that Sanford is a very, *very* sailor-friendly town. We like having the Navy here with us. You Navy mates are a very welcome addition to our town."

I smiled. "I'm feeling it already, thanks."

Before the afternoon was gone I had signed an offer sheet to purchase a

1959 Triumph TR-3 Roadster that was sitting on Holler's "previously owned" lot. Morgenstern said that it was "A real creampuff."

*   *   *

Jack Morgenstern made most of his car sales over a 7 & 7 cocktail in any of the many bars and lounges from Deltona to Altamonte Springs. Most of the sales came from either the Fleet Reserve Branch Home out on Sanford's Highway 46 or from George's # 2 – more commonly known as the Drift Inn which was located on the state highway to Titusville. You could find Jack in either of those spots or the Caribe Lounge on any day, with a drink in front of him, pecking at the bar top with his fingers drawn like a woodpecker's beak to emphasize his point during one of his many bar conversations, always on the alert for a friend that might possibly need a transportation upgrade. Hell, if they didn't exactly need one at the time he'd work on convincing that person that they did. "Let's evaluate your transportation needs" preceded his sales argument. It usually worked.

Jack was a genuine character. Stories of his Seagrams-fueled adventures are too many for this brief remembrance. He was a genuine personality, a unique individual who, although he must have had bar tabs outstanding in all his favorite watering holes, was always welcome when he bellied up to the bar, ready to "evaluate" someone's transportation needs.

Jack Morgenstern died in June of 1983 while an in-patient in the Sanford Hospital. While the cause of death was not given if I were to guess I'd say that his liver finally threw in the towel. He was cremated shortly thereafter. His will expressed that his ashes be scattered over the dirt parking lot of the Drift Inn. That dirt parking lot was a temporary parking spot for many a transient vehicle that would stop for refreshment on the road to Titusville. It would not have taken long for his ashes have been distributed across Central Florida and perhaps farther.

He would have liked that.

*   *   *

Valdez hotel, Sanford, Florida

The Legacy of Agent Orange

Recently I drove down to Cape Coral to pay my final respects to Ron Gagnon, my friend of more than 35 years. Ron was a retired Navy Chief Petty Officer, Vietnam Swift Boat veteran, stock car racer and award-winning restorer of Vintage Chevrolet Corvettes. Ron was 63 years old.

I first met Ron in 1975. I was the Operations Intelligence Division Chief (Surface) aboard the soon to be decommissioned and scrapped World War II era aircraft carrier Franklin D. Roosevelt. "Rosie" was a sorry mess at the time. Aging and rusty, "Rosie" was hampered by a warped shaft that incapacitated one of her four large propulsion propellers, and yet the Navy had dictated that she would have to make two more Mediterranean cruises with the Sixth Fleet to bridge the gap until some of the newer nuclear-powered carriers became operational. To make matters even worse, the "Zumwalt" era was in full bloom. CNO Admiral Elmo Zumwalt had begun the Navy's slide into "social engineering." Hair and beard regulations were relaxed, and other new regulations designed to make Navy service more friendly and palatable to the young first enlistment sailor were issued. These regulations were not favorably received by many command and flag level officers in the fleet.

One afternoon while the ship was in port at Mayport, Florida I was sitting in the Surface Section of the ship's Combat Information Center commenting negatively on the sorry state of the torn and dirty working uniform of Seaman James P. Butler when a Petty Officer First Class walked up to me and introduced himself as Petty Officer First Ron Gagnon. He had recently reported for duty and the Operations Officer had assigned Ron to the Surface Warfare Team and told him to report to me. Upon introduction I learned that Ron had recently served in Swift Boats in Vietnam which immediately forged a bond between us as I had served in Vietnam in 1968 on Patrol Gunboats. Ron and I were the only two men in the division - including the officers - who had served in Vietnam. We decided to tighten up the Division and get these young sailors squared away. Ron became my Lead Petty Officer on the spot, replacing a gentle, bearded, largely ineffective Petty Officer named Mashtare.

Ron took no crap from the men in the Division, nor the junior officer that was the Navy's answer to what passed for a Division Officer in the Navy of 1975. I can specifically recall an incident when one of the junior Petty Officers went AWOL for 24 hours and returned, confident that a slap on the wrist and perhaps some Division restriction was all the punishment that he would receive. Ron gave the young man two options: be placed on report and go to Captain's Mast where he was sure to be busted to Seaman or to chip away the rust spots and re-paint the Number 3-gun sponson outboard by himself over his next liberty weekend. The junior Petty Officer grumbled that it was seaman's work, and not fitting for a rated man. Ron responded. "Fine. Go to Mast, get busted to seaman and when you return THEN you can paint the #$%&* sponson!" The petty officer agreed to spend his next liberty weekend chipping and painting.

Ron and I made the 1975 Mediterranean cruise together and we never missed a liberty port or a bar in that port. We were the only two that always went ashore in uniform. We were proud of our uniforms and what they represented.

We were shipmates.

*   *   *

I retired in late 1976. Thirty-four years passed before I saw Ron again. He was attending a Swift Boat Veterans Reunion in Jacksonville and while we had remained in touch by e-mail and Christmas greetings over the years I jumped at the chance to hook up with my old friend and relive those long-ago memories. And relive them we did!

Ron was in poor health, receiving full combat disability compensation. His kidneys were failing, he had advanced emphysema which later became lung cancer, heart problems and diabetes, all from the Agent Orange defoliant in use in Vietnam long ago that had killed and disabled so many of our own. While the body was humbled, his spirit was not. The fire was still in his eyes, the "can do" spirit still in his heart. He talked of his family, his Corvettes and the tasks and trials that lay ahead.

Ron died shortly thereafter.

Goodbye, my friend and shipmate Ron Gagnon, Chief Operations Specialist, United States Navy, Retired. Fair winds and following seas on your new journey.

* * *

US Navy Swift Boats on Patrol in Vietnam